WHAT PESI DID

WHAT PESI DID

A Surgeon's Story

Dr. Azmy Birdi

ISBN 13: 978-81-948149-0-0
ISBN 10: 81-948149-0-1

Printed in India and published by BUUKS.

Disclaimer

This book is based on the life and work of my father—Dr. Pesi Bharucha. The events are based on information supplied to me by various friends, colleagues, patients, and also anecdotes from my own memory. The exact events and how they took place have been fictionalised and imagined as they might have occurred.

I have tried to recreate events, locales and conversations from my memories of them. In order to maintain their anonymity, in some instances I have changed the names of individuals and places. I may have also changed some identifying characteristics and details, such as physical properties, occupations, and places of residence.

Dedication

I dedicate this book to my father's friend and patient

—Mr. Yezad Kapadia.

It is because of his patience, love, support, guidance, and comfort that I have been able to write this book. Shortly after starting on my manuscript, I was overcome with emotion at all the memories that it brought back. I was by no means the perfect daughter or the daughter my father might have wished for; I was full of regret and self-recrimination. It was Yezad Kapadia who helped me make sense of my reminiscences, offering to be another father to me, an offer I gratefully accepted. While Dr. Pesi Bharucha is Daddy, Yezad Kapadia is now my pappa.

I have been blessed to have two illustrious fathers—one biological and one who has taken on the role out of love. Both these men have lived good, decent, honourable lives. Both have excelled in their careers—one as a surgeon, the other as a metallurgical engineer par excellence. Both were blessed with open, enquiring minds, reading widely on varied subjects, and both have been the most unassuming, humble, and gracious people you could ever hope to meet.

The book is a tribute to my beloved Daddy and dedicated to my dearest Pappa.

Dr. Azmy Birdi

Yezad Kapadia

Table of Contents

Acknowledgements

MY SINCERE GRATITUDE to Yezad Kapadia, who encouraged, supported, and comforted me through the writing of this book. Also to Zavher Chowdhury and Shiraz Tata for their help with the section about their father—Dr. Noshir Piroshaw. Jamshed Surti and Jehangir Rustomji for their stories of my father's operative skills and Shenaz Mistry for sharing details about her father's burns. A big Thank You to Mr. S. Ramachandran whose encyclopaedic knowledge of the Tata group of companies and memory of my father and other Tata employees has been invaluable. Roshan Dastur helped to fill some of the gaps. A special mention must be made of Flavia Lasrado, daughter-in-law of Col. Lasrado and her daughter—Dr. Maya Lasrado, who took a cold call from a complete stranger saying she was the daughter of Dr. Bharucha from Jamshedpur and in addition to giving me access to their family albums have blessed me with their friendship.

Dr. Azmy Birdi

Foreword

Zarir Pesi Bharucha
DAD
"Doctor *Saheb*," as my father was called, was a well-known figure in Jamshedpur. My earliest memories of him are teaching me to swim at the Beldih Club; evening drives in his Ambassador car at Jubilee Park and, even today, the faint memory of him taking me for a joy ride in an ambulance!

My father came to Jamshedpur from the UK as a young surgeon in 1956. I never met my paternal grandparents, as they had passed on by the time I was born. My grandfather Behramsha Bharucha was an agriculturalist in Amalner, a small town in Maharashtra. Dad often proudly reminded me when passing by Marine Drive that his father had graduated from Wilson College in Mumbai at the turn of the century. An achievement in those days.

It was from this humble agrarian background that my father went to Boys Town school in Nasik, Grant Medical College in Mumbai, and on to the UK, where he accumulated all four FRCS degrees. Dad's journey from an agrarian background in rural Maharashtra to an English qualified and trained surgeon was truly momentous given the times.

I believe it was his humble background that moulded his personality and from where he imbibed the human qualities of kindness, compassion for the less fortunate, and public service, which endeared him to all he came in contact with. Such was his popularity in Jamshedpur that he was offered a ticket to contest a local election by a political party!

The episodes in his life chronicled by my sister reveal his measure as a man and an accomplished surgeon dedicated to serving his patients and the local community. It is my privilege to rediscover his innate goodness and the selfless service he rendered to all who sought his help.

Pesi with his son Zarir on his 1st birthday

1

The Train to Tatanagar

*Do not follow where the path may lead. Go
instead where there is no path and leave a trail.*

—*Ralph Waldo Emerson*

PESI SAT BACK in the train and closed his eyes. His sister
and her family had waved him goodbye at Bombay and he was
on his way to Jamshedpur (station code Tata, for Tatanagar).
He looked at his appointment letter, signed by Sir Jehangir
Ghandy, thanking him for accepting the position as Consultant
in General Surgery and Second Surgeon at the Tata Main
Hospital, Jamshedpur.

It was hard to believe that only a month ago, he had been
working in North Liverpool in England. "Eight years," he
thought. "I have been away from India for eight years." He
cast his mind back to that fateful interview in London with Sir

Cecil Wakeley, President of the Royal College of Surgeons of England, and began to reminisce.

Having graduated with his MBBS from Grant Medical College, Bombay, in 1944, he had originally specialised in Obstetrics and Gynaecology. His sister had died of peritonitis after a botched Caesarean section, leaving a newborn daughter. The pain of that loss still came over him in waves, even after all this time. "Plucked from life when she was scarcely more than a child herself," he thought. Khorshed had been just a year older than Pesi, and the two of them had been close. She had married on May 15, 1943 and she died just nine months later, in February of 1944, leaving her baby girl and a bereft Kavas grieving the loss of his wife. Pesi remembered weeping at her funeral; he was twenty-three years old. They were in the midst of World War II and he remembered thinking that it was as if someone had thrown a grenade on their family. It was his last year in medical school with the final MBBS exams scheduled for October of that year.

He had resolved to study obstetrics and gynaecology himself, to be a safe and competent surgeon so families were not devastated the way his had been. However, Colonel Spackman had put paid to that. Thinking of Colonel Spackman made Pesi smile. Colonel W.C. Spackman, appointed honorary surgeon to the King in 1944, had been his professor of midwifery and gynaecology at Grant Medical College and JJ Hospital. Pesi remembered him arriving for his ward rounds on a horse. "Baroocka," as he called Pesi, "Come here and smell this," he said. "This" being a gloved finger with which he had performed a vaginal examination. "You can often tell whether the lady has thrush or not, just from the smell". Pesi still winced thinking about that. Identification of vaginal discharges by their smell was not his forte and he felt that his metier lay elsewhere.

But Spackman had been a good surgeon and an excellent teacher, putting him through his paces, a firm but fair mentor, encouraging him to think of a surgical career.

World War II had resulted in advances in the field of neuro-surgery with the development of mobile neurosurgery units in Europe as well as in India. There was an acknowledgement that there was a shortage of trained neurosurgeons, and Pesi thought that this was what he would like to do. After a stint in General Surgery at JJ Hospital in Bombay, he decided to go to the UK for further experience. Both his parents had passed away and although his father had left a small amount of money for him, it was woefully inadequate. It was his older brothers—Padamji and Jehangir—who had pooled together their resources for his ticket and a little extra.

Those early days in England had been an education in so many ways besides just medicine. He had gone over by ship where, for the first time, he had used toilet paper!

Then, various positions from house officer and registrar to senior registrar and senior hospital medical officer, most recently at the United Liverpool Hospitals. He had taken his FRCS (Fellow of the Royal College of Surgeons) four times over, in 1952 from Glasgow and then Edinburgh and then in 1954 from England (London) and finally in Ireland later that same year.

Neurosurgery had been depressing. The results of the oper-ations he performed upset him and resulted in introspection and reflection on the nature of the work he was doing and, more importantly, on the effect it had on patients. Prefrontal lobot-omy for "incurable" mental illness stripped patients of their personality and, often, independence. Removing brain tumours often resulted in survivors having epilepsy, losing their sense of taste, smell, and memory—people stripped of their identity and families, fearful and devastated by this transformation. It was the era of the general surgeon who could save life by removing an inflamed appendix or a gangrenous gall bladder or a twisted and obstructed intestine—and this was rewarding. This was what he had become a doctor for. To improve life, to save it in order for it to be worth living, and to be able to feel that his craft and skill was actually employed for the benefit of the patient.

The long hours did not bother him and he thought fondly of his landlady, Florrie. She always had a meal ready for him in the oven, however late he returned. Often, when he was delayed operating, he would request a colleague to phone Florrie. "Tell Florrie I am delayed," he would say. Bless her, Florrie always had something warm in the oven waiting for him when he finally got in. Who was going to cook for him now, he wondered. He could scramble an egg and often, the Indian doctors would make a curry in the hospital mess or at home when they got tired of bland food, but there had always been breakfast in hospital and if nothing else, tea on the wards and in the operation theatre. Apparently domestic staff were easily available in Jamshedpur. "I must get a cook cum houseboy," he thought.

Sir Cecil Wakeley (president of the Royal College of Surgeons of England) had been the examiner for his FRCS in London. He was impressed by the keenness and aptitude of this bright young surgeon and when Sir Jehangir Ghandy wrote, asking for him to recommend "a first class surgeon" for the Tata Main Hospital in Jamshedpur, Sir Cecil in turn wrote to Mr. Hunter in Liverpool, asking for his opinion on the "young Indian chap, I examined not so long ago."

Back came the reply . . . "He is a first-class surgeon both as regards clinical work and operative ability . . . I consider him one of the best surgical registrars I have ever had."

Pesi had been in two minds about returning to India. He had applied and been accepted for a post as a surgeon in America (the United States of America) but post independence India seemed exciting—he had a chance to go back and influence things, to make his mark professionally. He had agreed and received a fond farewell from his colleagues and staff, with whom he had been exceptionally popular.

He wondered what Christmas would be like. In England, the senior registrar, along with the registrar and matron, would carve the turkey on the ward for the patients who happened to be staying there during the festive season. And there was always a pre-Christmas gig at the hospital—some performance that the doctors would give for the rest of the staff followed by a Christmas meal.

Resting back in his seat, he opened a book and resigned himself to another thirty-two hours before the train reached Tatanagar.

Pesi in the CCF WWII

Pesi's eldest brother Padamji Bharucha

Pesi studying for his Primary FRCS

Pesi in his room Walton General Hospital Liverpool 1951-1952

Pesi - Walton General Hospital Liverpool

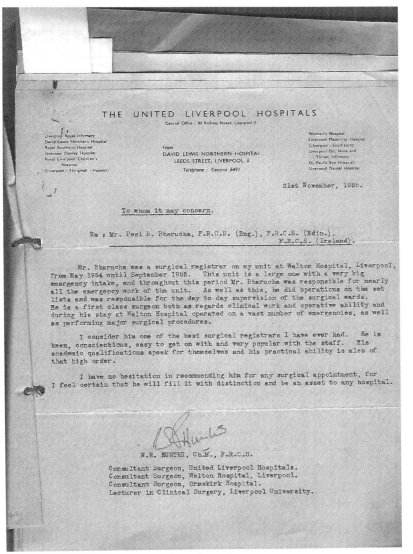

THE UNITED LIVERPOOL HOSPITALS

Central Office : 80 Rodney Street, Liverpool 1

Liverpool Royal Infirmary
David Lewis Northern Hospital
Royal Southern Hospital
Liverpool Stanley Hospital
Royal Liverpool Children's Hospital
(Liverpool : Thingwall : Heswall)

From
DAVID LEWIS NORTHERN HOSPITAL
LEEDS STREET, LIVERPOOL 3
Telephone : Central 6491

Women's Hospital
Liverpool Maternity Hospital
(Liverpool : Southport)
Liverpool Ear, Nose and Throat Infirmary
St. Paul's Eye Hospital
Liverpool Dental Hospital

21st November, 1965.

To whom it may concern.

Re : Mr. Pesi B. Bharucha, F.R.C.S. (Eng.), F.R.C.S. (Edin.),
F.R.C.S. (Ireland).

Mr. Bharucha was a surgical registrar on my unit at Walton Hospital, Liverpool, from May 1954 until September 1955. This unit is a large one with a very big emergency intake, and throughout this period Mr. Bharucha was responsible for nearly all the emergency work of the unit. As well as this, he did operations on the set lists and was responsible for the day to day supervision of the surgical wards. He is a first class surgeon both as regards clinical work and operative ability and during his stay at Walton Hospital operated on a vast number of emergencies, as well as performing major surgical procedures.

I consider him one of the best surgical registrars I have ever had. He is keen, conscientious, easy to get on with and very popular with the staff. His academic qualifications speak for themselves and his practical ability is also of that high order.

I have no hesitation in recommending him for any surgical appointment, for I feel certain that he will fill it with distinction and be an asset to any hospital.

W.R. HUNTER, Ch.M., F.R.C.S.

Consultant Surgeon, United Liverpool Hospitals.
Consultant Surgeon, Walton Hospital, Liverpool.
Consultant Surgeon, Ormskirk Hospital.
Lecturer in Clinical Surgery, Liverpool University.

Testimonial - A first class surgeon

Christmas as Senior Registrar on the ward

No.13/ 14 89   of 1948.
Office of the Principal,
Grant Medical College,
Bombay,   February, 1948.

This is to certify that Dr.Pesi Behramsha
Bharucha,M.D.(Bom), has been known to me, as a student
of the Grant Medical College and the J.J.Group of
Hospitals,Bombay, He took the degrees in Medicine and
Surgery of the University of Bombay, in October,1944,
passing the examination for the degree at the first
attempt. He passed all the three examinations for
the degrees in Medicine and Surgery at the first
attempt.

After qualification he held the following
appointments:-

1.House Physician,J.J.Hospital,Bombay,from 1-2-45
to 31-7-1945.

2.House Surgeon,Bai Motlibai & Petit Hospitals
Bombay,from 1-8-1945 to 31-1-46 and 1-3-1946 to
31-8-1946.

He passed diploma examination in Gynaecology
and Obstetrics of the College of Physicians and -
Surgeons,Bombay, held in April,1946,at the first -
attempt.

He also passed the Examination for Doctor's
Degree in Medicine(Midwifery and Gynaecology) of the
University of Bombay, in April,1947, at the first
attempt.

After taking Doctor's degree he has worked
as House Surgeon,J.J.Hospital,Bombay,from 1-8-1947 to
31-1-1948 for the Master's degree in Surgery.

He is well above average in his professional
ability and makes a pleasant colleague.

It gives me much pleasure to testify to his
good character and conduct.

Principal,Grant Medical College &
Superintendent,J.J.Group of
Hospitals,Bombay.

YAW.5/2.

University of Bombay

No. 363

I CERTIFY THAT

Pesi Behramsha Bharucha

passed the M. D. Degree Examination

held by the University of Bombay

in the month of May 1947.

Bombay

4 JUL 1947

for Registrar.

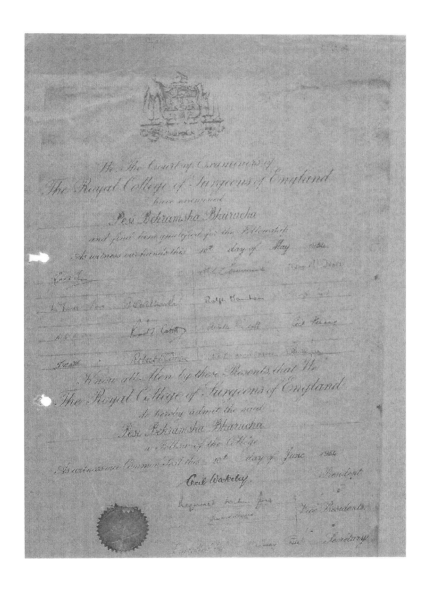

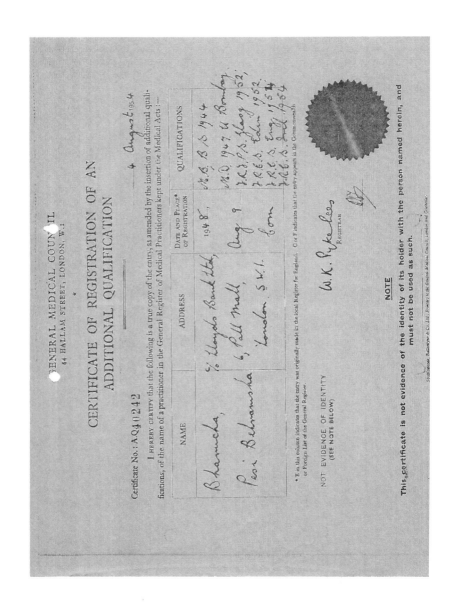

GENERAL MEDICAL COUNCIL
44 HALLAM STREET, LONDON, W.I

*

CERTIFICATE OF REGISTRATION OF AN
ADDITIONAL QUALIFICATION

Certificate No.: A.Q4()242 ———————— 4 August 1954

I HEREBY CERTIFY that the following is a true copy of the entry, as amended by the insertion of additional qualifications, of the name of a practitioner in the General Register of Medical Practitioners kept under the Medical Acts :—

NAME	ADDRESS	DATE AND PLACE* OF REGISTRATION	QUALIFICATIONS
Bhamela, Pesi Behramsha	c/o Lloyds Bank Ltd., 6, Pall Mall, London, S.W.I.	1948, Aug 9 Bom	M.B. B.S 1944 M.D. 1947 U Bombay, I.C.I.P.s. Glasg 1952, I.R.C.S. Edin 1952, I.R.C.S. Eng 1954, I.R.C.S. Eng 1954

* E in this column indicates that the entry was originally made in the local Register for England. Or F indicates that the entry appears in the Commonwealth
or Foreign List of the General Register.

W. K. Pyke Lees
REGISTRAR

NOT EVIDENCE OF IDENTITY
(SEE NOTE BELOW)

NOTE

This certificate is not evidence of the identity of its holder with the person named herein, and
must not be used as such.

Southwood, Baltantyne & Co. Ltd., Printers to the General Medical Councils, London and Colchester.

14

On holiday in Egypt

(Senior Registrar in Liverpool) Christmas gig 1955

NORTH LIVERPOOL HOSPITAL MANAGEMENT COMMITTEE

TELEPHONE: AINTREE 3611.
ALEXANDER SKENE.
M.B.E. M.B.Ch.B. M.R.C.P. (ED.)
PHYSICIAN SUPERINTENDENT.

Your Ref. ....

Our Ref. ....

WALTON HOSPITAL,

10th January, 1956.   **LIVERPOOL 9.**

Mr. Pesi Behramsha Bharucha, M.B.A., M.D., B.S.,
F.R.C.S.(Ed., Eng., and I.), F.R.F.P.S.

    Mr. Pesi B. Bharucha was appointed a Surgical Registrar to this hospital in May 1954, and held the appointment until leaving to return to India in September 1955.

    It early became apparent that the hospital had acquired a surgeon whose practical capabilities in the wards, operating theatres and clinics equalled his outstanding academic distinction.

    The surgical practice of this, the largest general hospital in England (1,321 beds), is varied and profuse, and Mr. Bharucha has had the fullest responsibility for the care of every type of surgical case, carrying out, on his personal responsibility, every variety of emergent and elective operative surgical procedure. I am very well aware that throughout the period of his appointment, Mr. Bharucha enjoyed the complete confidence of his senior surgical colleagues.

    When Mr. Bharucha joined the staff, undergraduate surgical clinics were seconded to the hospital from the United Liverpool Hospitals, and he undertook teaching duties, in association with his chiefs, with great acceptance. Since then, clinical Post-graduate classes have been regularly held, to which he has contributed very successfully.

    Mr. Bharucha has won the admiration and respect of his medical and nursing colleagues, and is well liked by them; he enjoys the full confidence of his patients.

    I have personally found Mr. Bharucha a loyal and charming colleague, and can unhesitatingly recommend him for a senior appointment, in the knowledge that he will bring distinction to it.

H. Skene

Consultant Physician Superintendent

Testimonial from Superintendent of North Liverpool Hospital

Return to India 1956 - Pesi getting off the ship

NG/RMG

10th November 1955.

Re Pesi Behramsha Bharucha Esq.,
NMs., M.B., B.S., M.D., F.R.F.P.S., (Edin)., (Glas)
F.R.C.S., (London).

Mr Pesi B.Bharucha was my Registrar from 16th May 1954
to 30th September 1955, and I have great pleasure in writing
this testimonial for such a valued colleague.

There is no need for me to stress his academic distinction
as his degrees speak for themselves. From the practical point
of view he has had an enormous and varied experience in this
hospital, which is the largest general acute hospital in England.
He has shared in the care of well over one hundred beds, and as
half of the admissions are of emergency character, he has had
plenty of experience in this field. I came to be able to place
great faith in his clinical judgement and I was soon able to leave
him to carry out major surgical operations without supervision.
Although it is not a teaching hospital, our unit does in fact
undertake Post-Graduate instruction both officially and un-
officially. Mr Bharucha has shown himself to be a keen teacher
and he has undertaken instruction classes in the wards and elsewhere outside the normal working hours and of his own volition.

He has got on very well with his colleagues both medical
and nursing, and is highly thought of by many people who were
patients under his care.

In conclusion I can only say I would be very happy to have
him working with me at any time in the future, and I feel sure that
he will make a great success of his surgical career wherever he may
settle.

Norman Gibbon.
Ch.M., F.R.C.S., (Edin)., F.R.G.S.,
Consultant General Surgeon.

18

NORTH LIVERPOOL HOSPITAL MANAGEMENT COMMITTEE

TELEPHONE: AINTREE 3611.

ALEXANDER SKENE.
M.B.E., M.R.C.B., M.R.C.P. (ED.)
PHYSICIAN SUPERINTENDENT.

Year Ref. ....

Our Ref. ....

WALTON HOSPITAL,

LIVERPOOL 9.

26th September 1955

THIS IS TO CERTIFY that Mr. Pesi B. Bharucha has performed the following operations at Walton Hospital during his stay from 16th May 1954 to 26th September 1955:

Appendicectomy	249
Inguinal herniae	122
Strangulated inguinal herniae	18
Femoral herniae	20
Strangulated femoral herniae	8
Umbilical hernias	11
Strangulated umbilical herniae	3
Incisional herniae	3
Strangulated incisional herniae	6
Perforated gastric and duodenal ulcers	59
Sub-phrenic abscesses	5
Laparotomy for intestinal obstruction	72
Varicose veins	53
Haemorrhoids	62
Hydroceles	5
Cysts of the epididymis	5
Epididymectomy for tuberculosis	1
Orchidopexy	2
Pilonidal sinus	2
Nephrectomy	3
Uretero-lithotomy	3
Wilson-Hey Prostatectomy	7
Freyer's Prostatectomy	2
Supra-pubic cystostomy	11
Gastrostomy	1
Gastro-enterostomy	1
Jejunostomy	2
Gastrectomy	15
Total gastrectomy, spleneotomy & cholecystectomy	1
Gastro-enterostomy and vagotomy	14
Cholecystectomy	30
Resection of Colon	7
Resection of colon with spleen	1
Closure of colostomy	8

/Over

19

```
Perineal end of synchronous )-  -   -   -  5
Combined resection of rectum)

Radical Mastectomy  -   -   -   -   -   -  1
Simple mastectomy   -   -   -   -   -   -  3
Phrenic crush       -   -   -   -   -   -  5
Bronchial cyst      -   -   -   -   -   -  2
Thyroglossal cyst   -   -   -   -   -   -  1
Amputation of thigh -   -   -   -   -   -  10
Skin grafting       -   -   -   -   -   -  5
Lumbar sympathectomy -  -   -   -   -   -  1
```

The above list does not include routine operative procedures such as cystoscopy, ureteric catheterization, sigmoidoscopy, excision of anal fissures, fistulae, removal of swellings, ganglia, radical toe nail operations, etc.

Norman Gibbon.

NORMAN GIBBON, Ch.M., F.R.C.S.(Edin.).,
F.R.C.S.

Consultant Surgeon

2

Second Surgeon at Tata Main Hospital— The Early Years

PESI WAS ASSIGNED a charming two-bedroom bunga-low with a lovely garden. He found Jamshedpur a well-planned town, designed as it was according to Sir Jamshetji Tata's instructions: "Be sure to lay wide streets planted with shady trees, every other of a quick-growing variety. Be sure that there is plenty of space for lawns and gardens. Reserve large areas for football, hockey and parks . . .

Colonel Lasrado, the first (chief) surgeon and Head of Tata Main Hospital (TMH) was warm and welcoming to the new incumbent. Albert Francis Lasrado was a military surgeon. After graduating from the Madras Medical School in 1928, he went to the UK where he obtained his MRCS and FRCS in 1932. He was the first Indian Christian to be awarded the FRCS from London. During World War II, he joined the army and ended his career as a Lieutenant Colonel. After the war, he came to Jamshedpur.

He had a gruff manner, but was a skilled and competent surgeon, always making the care of the patients and the welfare of the hospital his first concern. His wife, Blanche, and he often invited "Payzee," as the colonel insisted on calling him, to their home for a meal. Blanche had been born and raised in Ireland and was an excellent cook. She started making her Christmas pudding six months ahead, soaking the dried fruit in alcohol for several days and then hanging it up in a cool place for the flavours to settle. Blanche maintained that the best Christmas puddings were always aged and once, when she was pregnant and could not find the time, had to serve a "fresh" preparation, made only six weeks in advance.

Pesi was grateful for the experience he had gained in the UK, managing the largest emergency unit in the country.

He found that his role in the hospital was not just confined to surgical outpatient clinics and operating on patients. Tata had a rigorous recruitment system for their employees, who had to be physically strong in order to work on the shop floor. The heat within the steel plant and factory could be challenging to a person's stamina, and the doctors in TMH had a big role in screening employees.

In 1948, Colonel (Dr.) Najib Khan was Physician in Charge of the TMH and, along with two of his colleagues, had established a scientific forum in Jamshedpur for sharing case reports and teaching sessions in industrial medicine. The Society for the Study of Industrial Medicine (SSIM) was officially inaugurated in July 1948 (it is now called the Indian Association of Occupational Health).

The steel factory was in the middle of nowhere; the township had sprung up around it and in order to provide quality health care for the employees, Tata Main Hospital came into being. It had been established as a temporary hospital within a tent in 1908. An outpatient building as well as a general ward were constructed in 1922. X-rays were introduced between 1932 (when the radiology department was created) and 1935.

Tata Steel had set the bar high; the hospital had to provide the highest standards in clinical medicine, hygiene and sanitation, and grow in keeping with modern standards in order to provide comprehensive health care for their employees. Nursing and staff and other health care professionals were needed for the expansion of the hospital and, in 1933, a nurses' hostel was constructed followed by a formal School of Nursing in 1939. By 1950, TMH had over 400 beds and they had started speciality clinics in general medicine, tuberculosis, surgery, and dentistry.

The factory itself was a big complex, so health centres were needed within the steel plant itself; these came under the auspices of TMH, with first aid being administered at the plant. The patient would then be sent on, if necessary, to the main hospital, which was five miles away. Disposal of hospital waste was a big project, with incineration being the responsibility of TMH.

As second in command to the chief, Pesi soon realised how much effort it took to keep the hospital running smoothly. This included purchase and storage of medical supplies, distribution to various departments, monitoring of storage conditions, along with categorisation and itemisation.

Pesi was young, enthusiastic, and passionate about his work. On a typical day, he would start his ward rounds by 8:00 a.m., seeing patients and performing operations all day. He usually went home for his dinner at around 6:00 p.m. and then would be back again in the hospital for his night rounds. He was always courteous to the patients as well as his colleagues and other hospital staff, offering help without hesitation.

Dr. Chattoraj, currently a doctor at TMH himself, recalls his first encounter with Dr. Bharucha. There was a patient who had collapsed, and the medical team was struggling to put in a central line. A central line refers to a cannula placed in a large vein in the neck or chest, which allows fluid to be given rapidly. The doctors had been unable to get intravenous access when Pesi arrived for his night round. He offered to try, and Dr. Chattoraj, who was a newly qualified intern at the time, was amazed at the speed and skill with which Pesi located the subclavian vein just near the collar bone, before putting in the cannula and stitching it in place.

Colonel Lasrado, who was himself a strict disciplinarian from his many years of war service, was impressed with Pesi's dedication to his work as well as his clinical acumen and surgical skill. He often took late night rounds of the hospital himself and was at first pleasantly surprised to find Pesi in the hospital. Later, it gave him a sense of relief that there was someone he could rely on completely.

It was in the early days that the colonel asked Pesi if he could examine a nine-year-old child—a girl on whom a bronchoscopy had been performed. A bronchoscope is an instrument with a light, which is passed through the mouth into the trachea, to look inside the lung airways. After the procedure, the patient had difficulty breathing, and had pain in her chest along with retching. The medical team had been treating her conservatively, but she did not improve, and the colonel felt a second opinion was necessary. After Pesi reviewed the patient, he ordered an X-ray of her chest and abdomen. His suspicion that the girl's oesophagus (food pipe leading to the stomach) had been perforated during the bronchoscopy was confirmed when the images showed air under the diaphragm. A perforation (hole or rupture) of the oesophagus can be treated with surgery, repairing and closing the perforation, and draining the chest cavity, but this is likely to be successful if done in the first twenty-four hours of the original injury. Even so, the risk of dying can be as high as 25 percent, but this rises to 60 percent if treatment is delayed, as it was in this case. However, it is uncertain whether operating on a delayed or missed rupture of the oesophagus is likely to benefit a patient, and is controversial. When Pesi explained this to Colonel Lasrado, he exploded in indignation at the doctors who had performed the bronchoscopy. "I am going to catch them by the ba**s till they froth from the mouth," he fumed. Unfortunately, the child eventually died and her father gave a black-and-white photo of his daughter to Pesi, who was humbled by the man's attitude. Pesi had looked after the little girl for several days and had spoken regularly to the parents. He was devastated by her death and the fact that it was preventable.

He approached Colonel Lasrado, asking if he might review patients who had been scheduled for any type of procedure in TMH, both before or after they had undergone any treatment. This way, he felt there was a chance that incidents such as these could be prevented. Colonel Lasrado was delighted. Every night, Pesi and he would review the theatre list together, looking through X-rays, and would re-examine patients if necessary, discussing cases and ensuring that they had been diagnosed correctly and were receiving appropriate treatment.

On one occasion, Pesi noticed a patient had been listed for a zygoma lift. The zygoma is the cheekbone, and the zygoma lift is surgery for a fractured cheekbone. Looking at the X-rays, he realised that the temporozygmatic suture (the suture line between two parts of the bone) had been mistaken for a fracture.

He discussed it with the dental surgeon who had seen the patient; his colleague realised his error but requested that the surgery go ahead as it would result in loss of face. Pesi persuaded him that this was not ethical; instead he suggested that they could say that after discussion they had come to the conclusion that surgery was not necessary.

Besides the usual, appendicitis, hernias, and intestinal obstruction, there was a fair bit of trauma work. There was no orthopaedic surgeon in TMH at the time and fractured hips, shoulders, and wrists were something Pesi encountered on a regular basis. TMH being the main hospital for miles around, any cases of stabbing or gunshot injuries were also sent to the casualty. On one occasion, Pesi remembered with much gratitude his previous boss—Mr. Hunter, in Liverpool. Stab wounds of the buttock, resulting in penetrating injury, were not common, but Mr. Hunter had always insisted that a rectal examination be performed in every case. His experience in the war had taught him that often a penetrating wound of the buttock could result in a rectal tear, and to miss this could be fatal for the patient. Pesi had dealt with several penetrating stab wounds to the buttock, faithfully performing the PR (per rectal) examination in every case, but this was invariably normal, and privately he had wondered if this was perhaps just an unnecessary obsession on Mr. Hunter's part. Then, during a busy on call one night, a man was brought into casualty with a stab injury to his buttock. Out of sheer habit, Pesi followed his examination through with the obligatory rectal exam that old man Hunter had always insisted on and, to his shock, he discovered a tear of the rectal wall.

Excitedly, he wrote to his friends Sheila and John Mason, who had been his colleagues in England. Sheila and John were both doctors; John had done his surgical training with Pesi under Mr. Hunter and Sheila had chosen general practice. Sheila and John had married just before Pesi had left for India and they had decided to work in Africa, moving to Rhodesia around the same time that Pesi arrived in Jamshedpur. He wondered how they were getting on as a married couple and whether they'd had their first argument. He told them about his cook cum house keeper, who had the unlikely name of Aladdin. Aladdin was a law unto himself, and if Pesi did not check on the housework, he cut corners, which was irritating. Initially tolerant, Pesi realised that kindness was taken for weakness and periodically gave Aladdin a dressing down. This was borne with good grace by Aladdin, who remained cheerful but unrepentant. As Pesi wrote to his friends, he wished that instead of Aladdin, he could have a magic lamp instead to summon a genie who would do his bidding.

He posted this long letter, a detailed chronicle of his first impressions, the early days, his highs and lows as a second surgeon, and waited for a reply.

Box 119
Fort Jameson
1.5.57

My dear Pesi,

Just to show you we haven't forgotten you & to thank you for your letter of now so many months ago. You will note we have moved since last you wrote & are in a much prettier (hilly) part of Africa—though 400 miles at least from "civilisation". The hospitals here are continually running out of penicillin, strep gauze & cotton wool, Anti–malarials etc:—which makes treatment a little disjointed at times!!—however we get by!!!

How are you old lad?

How is India?—hope you've settled down & not got so homesick for W.Infirmary that you've applied to go back!

Are you married yet?

You seem to have had the same servant problem as we do—no supervision & little gets done—but by now I suppose you will have organised them rather better.

Everyone here seems divided into 3 groups—sporting types—the drinking types (apart from those that do both!) & the recluses! We have a large Indian population—stores & shopkeepers, but they think that I am too young!!!!! All I've had in that line was a youngster with an orange pip up his nose which I removed—a la Mr Hunter!—remember him!!

Well Pesi—Sheila wants to say a few words of greeting too so - - <u>do</u> keep in touch.

Kindest greetings to you—come & see us sometime—you old gay bachelor!—Yours <u>John.</u>

Dear Pesi,
What a funny letter John has written.

Well how's India, just as hot as Africa I expect, I can stand the mornings but o boy do the afternoons wear me out.

We are living at the moment in a dear little thatched house which is falling down, and being eaten away by white ants at the same time. But the thing that bothers me Pesi, is that we have to trip down the garden to a bucket to commune with nature.

We are both working at the African hospital at present, and I'm afraid neither of us understand the African mind, and the attitude, if they're going to die, well they can't stop them. I (sic) getting more used to it now.

Yes, in answer to your query John and I have quarrelled a few times, but you'll be relieved to hear, we are quite friendly at present. I don't know whether he is regretting losing his bachelorhood yet, my objection to marriage is that we never seem to have any money I think John must drink it all, any way he hasn't bought me a fur coat yet or any diamonds at all. Taken care of yourself and write when you've time.

Airmail letter from North Rhodesia

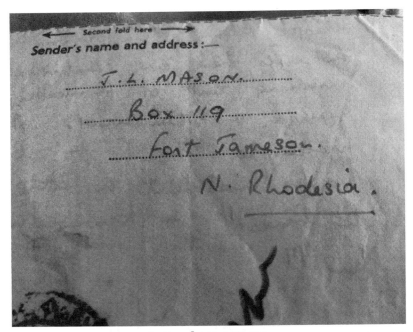

Letter from J Mason

The other problem was language. After spending a number of years abroad and communicating solely in English, he found that his Hindi, which had never been particularly good, was extremely rusty, and he struggled to make himself understood to patients who could not speak English. The staff at TMH were extremely willing to act as interpreters. However, effective communication is a key component of the doctor-patient relationship, and he knew that if it was not optimal, it could directly impact on patient safety, as patients often withheld sensitive information if they had to communicate via a third party. He needed to be able to listen to the patient's worries and, in turn, to explain to them the diagnosis and treatment options in a language that could be easily understood.

After making some enquiries, he found a Hindi tutor, who would come to the house twice a week and help him with colloquial and conversational Hindi. Pesi kept a small notebook in which he would make entries about terms that he needed to check on, and his teacher would talk him through this. The two men often spent time in role play to improve Pesi's consultation skills in Hindi.

Picture of Tata Main Hospital

3

Lt. Col. Dr. Albert Francis Lasrado

DR. LASRADO WAS born on April 10, 1904 in Mangalore, India. He was the second son of Gregory Stany and Christina Frances (Pinto) Lasrado. He was baptised in the Church of Our Lady of Miracles (Milagres Catholic Church), which the family attended throughout his youth.

Dr. Lasrado's medical career began in India after graduating from Madras Medical School. He did his MBBS there and received the Maharaja Gold Medal. Then he went to London to earn his FRCS in 1934. In the spring of 1935, he was told about a Catholic Indian family who lived in Waterford, Ireland. He visited Dr. Abundius d'Abrue and his wife Lucy (D'Souza) and liked them very much. He asked Dr. d'Abrue for the hand of his daughter in marriage. Then he returned to India to prepare for the arrival of his future wife. He arranged for her passage on a ship to Bombay. But he was very surprised when Blanche Teresa (the second oldest daughter, age seventeen) walked off the ship, instead of the oldest daughter that he was expecting! Blanche lived with the Lasrado family and got to know them and learn some of the Indian customs until she and Albert were married on November 20, 1935.

Albert and Blanche had five children: Germaine Sarojeni (Lasrado) D'Souza (living in Rio de Janeiro, Brazil), Adrian Francis (deceased on April 22, 2020 in Wallington, England), Dr. Gregory S. (deceased on February 18, 2014), Anthony David (living in Mason, Ohio, USA), and Christina Anita Lasrado, Doctor of Veterinary Medicine (living in West Chester, Ohio, USA).

Dr. Lasrado worked for a time in Rajasthan for the Maharaja of Bikaner. When World War II broke out, Dr. Lasrado was inducted into the British Indian Army. He served near the front lines of Burma in the Mobile Field Unit, performing surgeries and treating wounded soldiers with limited supplies and equipment. Each time the lines moved, the Mobile Field Unit moved too. Blanche wanted to be near her husband, so she lived in English bungalows as close to the action as was relatively safe. Albert was only allowed a weekend furlough once every fortnight. Their children were enrolled in Catholic boarding school during that time. Dr. Lasrado was commissioned as Lieutenant Colonel and discharged with distinction at the end of the war. He was respectfully called "Colonel Lasrado" or "the Colonel" by others after that.

After the war, Dr. Lasrado worked in Hyderabad as Chief Medical Officer of Osmania General Hospital for the Nizam of Hyderabad. A friend, Dr. Razak, advised him to seek employment in a private organisation when it was apparent that, with the pending Independence of India, the environment in Hyderabad would be very tumultuous. Tata Iron & Steel Co. (TISCO) in Jamshedpur, India, needed his services and offered him the position of First Surgeon of Tata Hospital. When Dr. Lasrado started serving in the hospital, there were fewer than 100 beds. When he retired, there were about 1,000 beds, many in large wards and several in private rooms reserved for the executives and officials.

He served there for many years and was sought out for his surgical skills by people across India and from other countries. During his years there, he was known for his exacting standards, where he required each physician to perform his best.

Surgery was his life and required most of his time. He often worked for sixteen hours per day and performed up to ten operations in a day. At that time, the colonel was the only surgeon in the hospital. There were occasions when workers sought him at home in an emergency. He even performed minor surgery on a woman on the ping-pong table!

Because Tata was a growing company, with more and more workers being recruited, and therefore more accidents and patients needing surgery, Dr. Lasrado was instrumental in finding surgeons to join the staff. He also sought and encouraged younger nurses and doctors, who showed promise, to return for advanced medical and surgical studies. He convinced Tata to fund their studies. In exchange they would sign a contract to return to Tata for a fixed period of service (a form of Co-Op). This program led to dozens of men and women launching fruitful careers in the medical field.

He learned of Dr. Pesi Bharucha in Bombay. Bharucha had recently completed his FRCS from London. He invited Dr. Bharucha to visit the hospital in Jamshedpur and hired him to work there.

The Lasrados did quite a lot of entertaining. They had bedrooms and bathrooms added to their house so that they could house visitors and people working at Tata's, sometimes for only a month, or on occasion up to two years.

In spite of his hectic schedule, Dr. Lasrado did find time to spend with his children. He often took them into the jungle and taught them to care for and shoot a rifle. One night, that skill was needed when a rabid jackal entered their yard. His son Tony picked up the rifle and killed the animal before it could do any harm.

There's an interesting story regarding Tony. In 1975, Tony, was living in the US, married to an American. A doctor from India, Dr. Sakarin, was the obstetrician for Laurinne, Tony's American wife. It wasn't until Tony and Laurinne's daughter Marie was born that Dr. Sakarin met Tony for the first time. Seeing him, Dr. Sakarin asked if Tony was related to Dr. Albert Lasrado, since it was then obvious that Tony was from India and also had the same last name. After learning that Dr. Lasrado was Tony's father, he told Tony that Col. Lasrado had actually been the doctor who delivered him! He did *not charge* for Marie's delivery!

That same year, another man from India saw Tony in a store and kept staring at him. Feeling uncomfortable, Tony walked over to the man and asked if there was some problem. The man asked Tony if he was Dr. Lasrado's son, to which he replied, "Yes." Then he exclaimed, "That son of a b**ch was a hard slave driver!" Then he went on to explain that he had been one of the recipients of the funds given by Tata's, and that he was a doctor because of that. He was extremely grateful for the opportunity he had been given.

Dr. Lasrado retired from his position at the Tata Hospital in 1963 and moved to Bangalore, India. He continued to advise and consult with doctors who served the poor in that city on a pro bono basis. A new emergency room was dedicated at St. John's Hospital in Bangalore in memory of Dr. Lasrado.

Dr. Lasrado died peacefully in his garden on March 18, 2001 with his wife and daughter Germaine (Lasrado) D'Souza nearby.

On Dr. Lasrado's Requiem Mass card was an extract from the Bible, Book of Sirach, Chapter 38:

Honour the physician with the honour due him,

for the Lord created the physician that He might be glorified in His marvellous works.

By them (God) heals and takes away pain.

A relative wrote the following poem:

Many were the wounded
    your skilled hands cured.
Your healing touch the
    sick to life restored.
Rich or poor, it mattered
    not to you.
Of your dedicated service,
    each got his due.
Precious are the memories
    you have left behind,
Of someone so great,
    yet so humble and kind.

Col Dr Albert Lasrado and his wife Blanche

Col & Mrs Lasrado

4

Baptism by Fire

THE PHONE CALL came at midnight on January 31, 1957. Soli Dastur was the chief electrical engineer of TISCO (the Tata Iron and Steel Company) in the central engineering department.

There had been an electrical breakdown in the steel factory and Soli, as chief electrician, was called in to rectify the problem and restore power supply.

Three men from his department were already waiting in the "works," as the factory was referred to. The source of the problem had been identified as a short circuit, but to get to the fuse box, the men had to make their way through a narrow passage. It was dark, and each man had a lamp in their hand. Soli led the way, but the corridor they had to negotiate was so cramped that they had to move sideways. As Soli moved ahead, there was a sudden flash (later reckoned to be 1,000 volts) and his lamp caught fire. He dropped the lamp and turned to run, but the last man had panicked and turned. Being possessed of a stout frame he found himself wedged within the passage, holding up the exit of his colleagues. Help was at hand, but the width of the corridor did not permit a quick removal of the men. Soli and the man behind him were badly burnt. The brunt of the attack, however, was borne by Soli.

His son-in-law Firoze Mistry recalls:

It is not clear if it was a kerosene lamp but definitely not a petro-max . As far as i remember, part of the power was there and he had a hand lamp which had a bulb, connected with a long wire. When one gets a shock with ac type current, it clings onto you while as with old dc type it flings you.

Ac clings; dc flings. In the electrical lamp, the bulb is protected by a cage.

    The short circuit occured somewhere, somehow, and the cage stuck to soli's calf, and a brand in the shape of the lamp guard was burnt into his calf. This happened after the sudden high voltage flash, which was more than a 1,000 volts.

    Also, i would like you to add that generally, when anyone gets 30 percent burns of first degree, the chances are very less of surviving. But in soli's case, it was not first degree or second degree but third degree burns of 90 percent, which in itself is a miracle.

It was the early hours of the morning when Pesi received the call. There had been a "short" (short circuit) within the steel works and some people had been injured. They were being brought to TMH (Tata Main Hospital). Colonel Lasrado was away and Pesi was in charge as second surgeon. He had no idea of what he was about to deal with. Soli had third degree burns affecting 90 percent of his body surface area. Although experience in treating burns had advanced during World War II and Pesi had accumulated some experience in the treatment of burns while in the UK, he had never had to deal with such severe or extensive ones. The staff at TMH thought highly of Dr. Bharucha, but he had only started in post on the October 31 the previous year. Pesi had joked to his English colleagues that he was starting his new job on Halloween, but four months down the line he wondered if this had been a sign of things to come.

He remembered his boss saying that the mortality of burns is approximately equal to the total body surface area affected. "A 10 percent chance of survival," he thought.

Extensive burns do not just result in destruction of the skin and underlying tissue; they affect almost every organ of the body. Inflammatory substances released as a result of heat injury affect the lining of the gastrointestinal tract with the possibility of ulceration, result in reduction of blood flow to the kidney and renal failure, and breakdown of the skin barrier leads to loss of fluid and electrolytes from the body, which in turn affects cardiac function, and there is a high risk of sepsis.

The first step was to treat burns shock, which is due to the loss of blood plasma from the damaged skin and blood vessels. Third degree burns need skin grafting, but it was difficult to find any suitable skin due to the extensive nature of the burns. Soli's groin and part of his abdomen had been spared. Immediate intravenous resuscitation was started along with antibiotics to prevent sepsis. Soli's wife Nergish assured Pesi that her husband was not allergic to penicillin, and Pesi silently thanked God for small mercies. High protein nutrition had to be given via a nasogastric tube. Pesi was aware that Soli needed treatment in a specialised burns unit, but the nearest one was in Calcutta, and Soli's condition needed to improve before that could even be considered.

An isolation room was created especially for Soli. Only his wife was allowed to visit, and even she was only allowed to observe through the small window in the cabin door. The cleanliness and hygiene was maintained similar to that in an operation theatre, with all the doctors and nurses wearing sterile gloves and gowns, and a rota created for doctors and nurses to provide twenty-four-hour care on a one-to-one basis.

His daughter Shenaz recalls seeing him in hospital under a huge net and thinking, "No, this is not our Dad." The naked man covered in charred flesh bore no resemblance to the father she knew.

Immersion in a bath of sterile saline was performed regularly and, after the fifth day, Pesi began the process of removing some of the dead and charred skin and performed split skin grafting. In a few months, Soli was well enough to be moved to Bombay, where he remained for two years, undergoing several operations including grafts to his neck and eyelids.

"The miracle case," as everyone called it, attracted much interest and attention all over India, and Pesi was asked to speak on burns treatment at national conferences. Finally, on the April 9, 1959, Soli was discharged home from hospital. Thereafter, his family always celebrated two birthdays for him in a year. February 20—the day on which he was born, and April 9—the date of his final discharge.

Soli as a young man

Soli after retirement - he lived to
the age of 86

Soli's scars

5

Hand Over Fist

IT WAS THE spring of 1958. Minoo Rustomji was driving his fiancée Peggy around Jamshedpur. They were to be married in a few weeks and were excitedly discussing the guest list. The King of Sikkim was one of the guests. Minoo's brother Nari was the *dewan* (Prime Minister) of Sikkim and was close to the royal family.

They passed a gulmohar tree in flower, and Peggy asked Minoo to stop the car so they could take some photographs. For several weeks in March and April, the gulmohar trees blossom with exquisite flame-red flowers. Peggy was admiring the scarlet-orange blooms and wondering if they could have some for the wedding, rather than the traditional roses and lilies.

Suddenly, almost out of nowhere, three men appeared. One of them had a knife in his hand. Minoo took Peggy's hand to lead her back into the car, but the man moved swiftly in front of them, blocking the way and holding the knife aloft.

"*Paisa* (Hindi for money)," he said. Minoo had been educated in England, having done his schooling at Bedford College and moving on to the London School of Economics for his degree. He had come to Jamshedpur to take up a senior managerial position at TELCO (Tata Engineering & Locomotive Company, now Tata Motors). Hindi was not his forte, but he understood that the ambush was for money. "I say, old chap, I don't have my wallet on me," he explained, turning out his pockets to illustrate the point. The three men moved close, glaring balefully at the frightened couple, and the knife was raised menacingly. In desperation, Minoo held out both his hands, palms upward, stressing the fact that they were empty-handed. The man threatening them swore in frustration and brought the knife down in an arc towards Minoo's wrist. Peggy cried out in fright and instinctively put her right hand out to prevent the attack and then screamed as the blade sliced her palm. Their attackers fled, leaving Peggy collapsed in pain, blood flowing from her hand.

A distraught Minoo bundled her into the car, and drove straight to Tata Main Hospital. As luck would have it, Colonel Dr. Lasrado, first surgeon and chief of TMH, was in the hospital with Pesi, who was on call that day. Their presence was a great reassurance to the terrified young couple. Minoo's sister Thriti was married to Pesi's colleague—Dr. Fali Billimoria, a chest physician at the TMH. They had heard reports of the clinical acumen and skill of both surgeons, which they now experienced firsthand.

Peggy was given a pain killer, and a tourniquet (tight dressing to staunch the bleeding) was applied, elevating her hand above the level of her heart, after which the doctors began cleaning the wound and examining her hand, testing for sensation, blood flow, and movement of the fingers. Peggy had sustained a deep cut to her palm, severing the flexor tendons of her hand. Before a decision could be made about treatment, an X-ray was necessary to rule out a fracture of the bones of the hand.

As a result of the knife injury, the flexor tendons in Peggy's hand had been severed. The surgeons explained that the tendons are like rubber bands, connecting the muscles to the bones. They are taut and supple and if they are sliced apart suddenly and forcibly, the fingers can no longer bend and the function of the hand is lost. The tendon cannot heal unless the ends are brought together, which has to be done surgically.

By this time, the whole family, including Minoo's mother, had arrived at the hospital and everyone was keen that the operation be performed as soon as possible. They were told that the tendons might have been damaged in different ways—they may have been cut clean through or at an angle or pulled off the bone completely. As cut tendons tend to retract (shrink back), it would not be possible to decide without exploring the injury, which would involve opening the wound and examining the underlying damage under general anaesthesia. Peggy would need antibiotics and a tetanus shot.

In the operating theatre, the wound was carefully enlarged, taking great care not to jeopardise the blood supply to the skin flap. Unfortunately, the ends of the tendon had been rendered asunder at an angle, with the ends being so frayed, that primary repair by suturing the ends together was not possible.

Once Peggy had recovered from the anaesthetic and was back in the ward, Pesi explained the position and proposed taking healthy tendons from her foot and transplanting them to her hand. This seemed fanciful but Colonel Lasrado explained that tendon transfer operations had been performed for over a hundred years; Colonel Lasrado had performed this surgery for injured soldiers during the World War II, and Pesi had experience in performing this surgery for painful flat feet as well as for polio.

Two operations would be required for the tendon transfer. First, the injured tendon would need removal, followed by removal of a healthy superfluous tendon from Peggy's foot. The aim was to restore a stable and functioning right hand. Peggy would be in the operation theatre for about four hours and the risks of infection, nerve damage and haemorrhage were explained to her.

As Peggy signed the consent form, she told the surgeons, "Well, I suppose it will all depend now on Peggy's luck and your skill."

The operations went off smoothly, without a hitch. While it took a whole year for full recovery, Peggy was discharged in time for her wedding. The right arm, bandaged in a splint, was skilfully covered with a shawl for the wedding photographs and the king of Sikkim was the chief guest.

Peggy and Minoo on their wedding day, with the injured hand
covered with a shawl. The king of Sikkim looks on in the background.

6

An Inspirational Teacher and the Birth of the TMH Clinical Society

The mediocre teacher tells. The good teacher explains. The superior teacher demonstrates. The great teacher inspires.

—William A. Ward

PESI HAD ALWAYS enjoyed teaching; he had been a post-graduate teacher in surgery at the Walton Hospital, Liverpool, where he often quoted Socrates's famous saying, "I cannot teach anybody anything; I can only make them think."

TMH was not a teaching hospital when he was first appointed; there was no medical college in Jamshedpur, and because the posts in TMH were not recognised by any university as counting toward accreditation for postgraduate medical training, many bright young doctors had to leave for a bigger city in order to get a "recognised job." Pesi thought this was a great shame, because there was a wealth of experience to be obtained by working in TMH, and if they could get accreditation as a teaching hospital, they would be able to attract talented junior doctors who, after training, could be retained within the hospital. (To get an MS (Master of Surgery) or MD (Doctor of Medicine), a junior doctor must do three years of accredited or recognised posts; the recognition is awarded automatically to teaching hospitals. A postgraduate teacher is also required as an MD or MS degree in India requires the submission of a thesis or dissertation to the university, for assessment, along with the mandatory written and practical examinations).

In 1959, Dr. S. Pan approached Pesi. After his graduation and internship, Dr. Pan had worked briefly in TMH and Pesi's expertise had left a deep impression on him. Pesi had an FRCS degree from every one of the four Royal Colleges of Surgeons in England, Scotland and Ireland; could he not be his postgraduate teacher for the MS examination of the University of Calcutta? Pesi was unsure, as each university has their own panel of postgraduate teachers under whose supervision a candidate writes their dissertation, but Col. Lasrado was enthusiastic and wrote to the postgraduate examination division of Calcutta University, making a case for Pesi to be recognised as a guide for this candidate in respect to the dissertation and also for approval of the position in TMH. Pesi had gained a national reputation by then, especially after his treatment of Mr. Dastur, who had sustained over 90 percent burns a few years ago, and the University approved his application to be a postgraduate supervisor and guide for the MS examination.

Dr. Pan's dissertation on head injuries was duly submitted, and Pesi's first MS student passed his postgraduate exams in 1960.

In November of 1961, a medical college—Mahatma Gandhi Memorial Medical College (MGM)—was established, and Pesi was appointed director of Clinical Studies and head of the Department of Surgery.

When Dr. Pan had been working towards his MS qualification, Pesi would spend a couple of hours every week doing a practice viva voce (an oral examination conducted like an interview of knowledge and skills, which is part of an MS or MD exam in India), discussing cases, and guiding his student through the clinical examination. Other doctors in the hospital expressed an interest in attending these sessions and soon, the weekly clinical meeting was well attended and became a regular part of Pesi's schedule at the hospital.

In 1962, Dr. Dasgupta, who had trained as a surgeon, decided to specialise in obstetrics and gynaecology. He had watched in fascination as Pesi had performed a vaginal hysterectomy (removal of the uterus via the vaginal route, rather than making a cut on the abdomen) under local anaesthesia for an elderly lady with a prolapse of the uterus. (When the muscles and ligaments become so weak that they are no longer able to support the womb/uterus, it sags into the birth canal/vagina; this is referred to as a prolapse.) There was no senior obstetrician/gynaecologist at TMH at the time, and Dr. Dasgupta, who had always had a keen interest in women's health, felt that he would like to set up a worthy department.

The weekly clinical meetings were now formalised into what is still known today as the "Clinical Society" in TMH.

In 1963, Dr. K.N.A. Subramaniam and Dr. B.P. Sengupta were trained by Pesi for the MS exam (this time it was for the Bihar University). Dr. Subramaniam's dissertation was on anorectal abscesses and fistulae, and Dr. Sengupta's was on observations of fifty cases of haemorrhoidectomy. These were based on cases they had observed at TMH under Pesi's supervision.

In 1964, Dr. Dasgupta went to the UK for his MRCOG (Member of the Royal College of Obstetricians & Gynaecologists) qualification. While he was away, all emergency and elective C-sections were performed by Pesi. His original training as an obstetrician and gynaecologist stood him in good stead. The wife of one of the Tata directors recalled her first meeting with him when he was standing in as Chief of Obstetrics and Gynaecology at TMH. She was pregnant for the first time and seemed to be "showing" rather excessively. She had been to a doctor in Bombay, who examined her and said she was five months pregnant. "I can't be five months pregnant, Doctor," she protested. "I was not with my husband five months ago." The doctor held up his hands and said, "I don't know about all that; all I know is that you are definitely five months pregnant." Pesi palpated her abdomen carefully and at length; finally he said, "Ah, I can feel the second head," and then told her that she was carrying twins. The diagnosis proved correct when she delivered two boys four months later.

Pesi with colleagues

Pesi with Anaesthetists TMH

7

Barkis Is Willing

"Well. I'll tell you what," said Mr. Barkis. "P'raps you might be writin' to her?" "I shall certainly write to her," I rejoined. "Ah!" he said, slowly turning his eyes toward me. "Well! If you was writin' to her, p'raps you'd recollect to say that Barkis was willin'; would you?" "That Barkis was willing," I replied. "Is that all the message?" "Ye—es," he said, considering. "Ye—es; Barkis is willin.'"

—From David Copperfield *by Charles Dickens*

PESI WAS JAMSHEDPUR'S most eligible bachelor. Good-looking, polite, well-mannered, a highly skilled professional with an impeccable character, he was considered a catch. The older women schemed, the younger ones hoped, and several people connived to introduce him to "a suitable girl."

He had established a reputation as a top-class surgeon, on course to become the Chief Surgeon and Head of TMH, and there were several proposals of marriage which Pesi politely declined. He seemed to be wedded to his profession, spending long hours in the hospital. Veera and Jeelu Billimoria, who were studying at the Sacred Heart Convent school for girls in Jamshedpur, remember nicknaming him "The Virgin Pesi."

Sir Jehangir (Joe) Ghandy, the director in charge of TISCO at the time, teased Pesi about being a confirmed bachelor. Did Pesi already have someone he cared about or was he not interested in marriage, he wondered. Pesi replied that he was very interested in getting married, but had not found the right person yet. He had been introduced to many ladies but had never felt a strong attraction to any of them. He assured Sir Joe that when he did meet "the girl for me," he would indicate his interest by quoting the phrase from *David Copperfield*—"Barkis is willing." Barkis is a character in the book, and David travels in his wagon to and from school. He gets to know Clara Peggotty, who was housekeeper to the Copperfield family and proposes to her by sending a message via David: *"Tell her, 'Barkis is willin'!' Just so."*

Pesi carried on with his work, growing in stature and repute as a surgeon, but whenever Sir Ghandy asked him if Barkis was willing, the reply was, "Not yet, sir, not yet."

Then, in 1960, a young graduate, Khorshed Andhyarujina, arrived in Jamshedpur. The first female recruit of the prestigious TAS (Tata Administrative Service), she had been sent to work for a few months in TISCO, Jamshedpur, under Sir Jehangir Ghandy. Later, that year, Khorshed's eldest sister, Gool Andhyarujina, came to visit her. Gool was still unmarried at twenty-nine; she was a qualified lawyer, practising in the Bombay High Court. She was beautiful.

Sir Ghandhy hosted a dinner at his home one evening for Gool and Khorshed, inviting Pesi along. For once, Lady Ghandy was not trying to matchmake; a few days earlier, Pesi had mentioned that Aladdin, his cook, was on leave and she had suggested he come along for a meal.

The evening was a success, and Sir Joe and Lady Roshan could not help but notice that Gool and Pesi seemed to be getting on rather well together.

When he was leaving, Pesi shook Sir Ghandy's hand warmly and said with a smile, "Barkis is willing."

The young Pesi

Gool Andhyarujina December 1959

Pesi with Sir Jehangir Ghandy

Pesi & Gool newly engaged

8

Teething Problems

"DO YOU KNOW what they call you?" boomed Colonel Lasrado, glaring at the young dentist standing before him.

"*Paagal* Piroshaw, that's what they say." Before Piroshaw could reply, there was a knock at the door. "Come," snapped the Colonel, and Pesi entered.

"Ah, I was just telling Dr. Piroshaw that within less than a year of being in post, he has acquired a reputation of being *paagal*, crazy, mad. And you, Pesi, seem to be going the same way, from all accounts. Do you want to be a double act— *Paagal* Piroshaw and *Pagla* Pesi?"

Dr. Noshir Piroshaw had been appointed as a dentist at the Tata Main Hospital in Jamshedpur in January 1961. After qualifying as a dentist, he had been to Tufts Dental School in USA to study periodontology.

He spent two years with Dr. Irving Glickman, Chair of the Department of Periodontology at Tufts, before returning to the UK. Dr. Glickman was well respected internationally and spent long hours working with patients and conducting clinical research under his mentorship.

In 1960, Dr. Piroshaw was working as professor and head of dentistry at Madras Medical College when he was offered a post at the Tata Main Hospital in Jamshedpur. Sir Jehangir Ghandy, the managing director of TISCO, had met Dr. Fali Mehta, a dentist in Bombay, and mentioned that the Tata Main Hospital was looking to recruit a good dentist. Dr. Fali Mehta said, "I have one in mind. Noshir Piroshaw. He may not be very good-looking, but as a dentist he is very good." And thus, Dr. Piroshaw was headhunted.

When Noshir arrived in Jamshedpur in January of 1961, his wife Sheroo was pregnant with their first child. Despite a ten-year difference in age, Noshir and Pesi bonded immediately as professionals. Often medical disorders can manifest in the mouth before being obvious elsewhere, e.g., inflammatory bowel disease, anaemia and other blood, autoimmune and infectious diseases.

As a trained periodontist with an excellent knowledge of other medical disciplines with which his own field overlapped, Noshir was often the first person to suspect, and often detect, the signs of a general disease, practising a truly holistic form of dentistry. Invariably he would request Pesi to see the patient, and they would perform biopsies on the cheek, mouth, and jaw, leading to patients being diagnosed with Crohn's disease, ulcerative colitis, diabetes, cancer, and leprosy.

The two men had more in common than just a passion for good medical practice. They were both self-made, having lost their parents at a relatively early age, and had no connections or contacts other than those made during the practice of their discipline.

Noshir's mother had died when he was very young. However, his *maami* (mother's brother's wife) who had been very close to her sister-in-law, became a mother figure to him after his *maama* (maternal uncle) brought him to their home in Surat after Noshir's mother passed. Noshir's father remained in close touch and Noshir was grateful for having his father as well as his *maami* always looking out for him. After completing his Inter Science (second year of University Science) in Surat, Gujarat, Noshir went on to study dentistry at Nair Dental School in Bombay. He was able to do this only because another relative—Mr. Dotivala in Bombay—welcomed him into their home in Rustom Baug, Byculla. They encouraged him in his studies, and his aunt and cousin would pack lunch for him to take to college every day. Noshir always had immense gratitude to this family for giving him a place to live as well as for the encouragement he received to further his career.

For Pesi, Noshir's arrival was like a breath of fresh air. It was stimulating and exciting to have a colleague who, having returned from a centre where cutting-edge research and techniques were in place, brought in new ideas and innovative practices. Up until that time, the dental department at TMH used autoclaving for sterilising the dental equipment. However, the autoclaving was performed in the main hospital, at some distance from the dental department. Waiting for an instrument going into the sterilisation phase resulted in loss of efficiency, and Noshir requested that the dental department be given its own autoclave so the sterilisation could be done in-house. In addition to this, he insisted that he would only use disposable needles for dental procedures. This created unrest among his own staff as well as those in other departments. They felt they had managed perfectly well before, and there was no need for such expense and trouble. While waiting for the hospital management to sanction his request, Noshir brought in disposable needles and syringes at his own expense from a local chemist. He convinced Pesi of the benefits of this, and the two of them decided to conduct a trial using disposable needles in one set of patients and the reusable variety in the other group. They kept meticulous records and a register of patients, staying on long after their patients and other colleagues had gone home.

There was displeasure among the staff at the changes introduced and that Dr. Bharucha, as senior surgeon, second to Colonel Lasrado, seemed to be so taken in with this new-comer. Numerous complaints were made to Col. Lasrado that the new dentist was crazy.

Col. Lasrado, despite his stern demeanour, was an immensely fair boss, supportive to his staff, and desired nothing more than to advance and improve the standard of medical care in TMH. He listened carefully and patiently as Noshir made his case. Autoclaving was widely used for sterilisation of instruments, but its efficacy had not been demonstrated for viruses. Because of the shape of hollow needles and the deposited debris in the lumen, the pathogenic viruses and bacteria are protected from the killing effects of high temperatures. The answer to this problem of uncertain sterilisation therefore lay in the routine use of disposable needles.

The trial conducted in the TMH dental department showed a much lower incidence of infection in the group treated using disposable needles. While the initial cost was higher, with the decline in infection rate and subsequent reduction in use of antibiotics, re-admissions, and time off work these eventually resulted in cost savings. Thus, within a year, single-use, disposable needles were in place and Dr, Piroshaw was no longer considered *"paagal."* He was meticulous about infection

control and insisted on complete asepsis within his department, training all his staff on the importance of hand washing
and sterilisation of instruments.

Noshir was unfailing polite and courteous to all his
patients, from the most humble labourer to the most senior
Tata directors. He always said that if the common man's wife
was not treated as you would treat the queen of England,
how would you know how to treat the queen of England, if
she happened to come.

One day, an employee brought his child to the dental
clinic. The child had a problem with his hearing but unfortunately, in those days, the ear plugs for hearing aids came in
adult sizes only. This child could benefit from hearing aids,
but there were no plugs that would fit him and he had been
excluded from school. Moved by the plight of this family,
Noshir offered to help. Within the dental department, the
team was making impressions and moulds for teeth. Noshir
offered to take an impression of the child's external ear and
auditory canal, experimenting with custom-made plugs. The
child was eventually fitted with his hearing aid and began
to attend mainstream school. For many years thereafter, the
dental department created bespoke earplugs for children
who needed hearing aids.

The following testimony speaks for his skills in dental surgery:

> It is not always that a dentist's chair scares patients. I know of at least one doctor, N.A. Piroshaw of the Tata Main Hospital, Jamshedpur, whose treatment was a pleasure. Whether he was extracting a tooth or filling a cavity, you would not know until the job was over and he told you to get up from the chair.
>
> All through the treatment, he would keep you engaged with his smiling and friendly talk.
>
> **N.S.R. Murty,**
> Secunderabad

Dr. Noshir Piroshaw ran the dental department at Tata Main Hospital for thirty-seven years. He was well respected as a dentist (many people, including Russi Mody, insisted he was the best dentist in the world) both in Jamshedpur and outside. When the Tata board meetings were held in Jamshedpur and the directors came from Bombay, many of them would book an appointment with Dr. Piroshaw for dental treatment, even though they had access to the best dentists in Bombay. He was passionate about teaching and training and set up a programme with Dr. Jorgen Theilade of the Royal Dental College in Aarhus, Denmark to train Danish dentists in TMH.

Pesi and Noshir remained life-long friends till they died within a year of one another.

from left Dr Reddy- radiologist, Dr Piroshaw - dental surgeon,
Dr Aggarwal -ENT surgeon, Dr Bharucha & Dr KP Misra -
general surgeon

Noshir & Sheroo Piroshaw

9

Riding the River

"What do you want in a woman, in life?"

*I thought a moment . . . The Rangers . . . we began
to describe one another in a few simple words:
El es muy bueno para cabalgar el rio. Meaning,
"He'll do to ride the river with." In Texan, it
means, "I'd trust him with my life."*

*I scratched my head. "I want someone to ride
the river with."*

—Thunder and Rain,
Charles Martin

PESI AND GOOL settled into married life after a honeymoon in Kodaikanal. Gool wound up her practice in Bombay and took a job with Tata Robins Fraser (TRF) shortly after its creation in November of 1962.

Pesi carried on with his work, which Gool was supportive of, never complaining about the long hours he spent away home. Later that year, Jamshedpur got its own medical school, and Pesi became the first Professor of Surgery.

In June of 1964, Col. Lasrado retired and Pesi was appointed Surgeon and Chief Superintendent of Tata Main Hospital. Gool was pregnant with their first child when they moved into their new home—2 BC Road. TMH was in the same lane, a drive of less than a minute. Pesi took over the role of director of Clinical Studies and head of the Department of Surgery at MGM Medical College. The hospital facilities in the Steel City were supplemented by dispensaries and clinics spread over the township, and he was also in administrative charge of these as well as the industrial medical department in the factory and the overall management of the Sir Ardeshir Dalal Hospital for chest diseases, where he was appointed director.

There was no training pathway for hospital administration at the time, no courses or associations; Pesi had to learn on the job. He had the respect and admiration of the hospital staff and, as he treated everyone from the cleaners to the top management with equal courtesy, he discovered the value of team work and synergy—the bonus that is achieved when people work together harmoniously.

The staff adored Pesi, and he commanded the loyalty of everyone from the doctors to the cleaners and watchmen. On one occasions, a mob of students staged a demonstration that got out of hand. The police beat them up and, in protest, students from the surrounding areas joined them. Hundreds of students went on a rampage, smashing shop windows and throwing stones. Word got around that they were headed for the hospital, and Pesi received instructions to lock the gates. The Pathan security guards advised him against this. They said that the locked iron gates would only serve to aggravate the miscreants, who would see the fact that they had been barred entry as a challenge to enter and return with reinforcements. The Pathans requested Pesi to allow them to manage the students and promised him that they would allow no harm to come to the hospital or any of the patients.

When the mob turned up at the gates, they were surprised to be greeted courteously with the guards offering them fresh drinking water. They were then told that the head of the hospital, Dr Bharucha, would meet them, so they trooped after the guards who led them through the maternity unit so they could see the newborn babies in their cribs along with their mothers. The students were asked if they really wanted to harm women and children. Having calmed down by then, many were feeling ashamed of themselves. When they saw Dr Bharucha, he courteously said, "*Namaste*," and asked what he could do for them. The ring leaders said, "*Namaste, kuch nahin, hum jaa rahe hain*" (nothing, we are going now) and the group left.

According to the 1965 Report of the Indian Commission of Jurists on Recurrent Exodus of Minorities from East Pakistan and Disturbances in India, thousands of Hindu families left East Pakistan and sought refuge in India after January 5. The Indian Government arranged for special trains to deliver them to the states of Bihar, Orissa, and Madhya Pradesh where they were to be received. As these trains crossed through Indian towns, the narrative of the atrocities that these migrants had suffered in East Pakistan spread, triggering communal riots. Jamshedpur (Bihar) and Rourkela (Orissa) were particularly affected. In Jamshedpur, violence flared up on March 19. The army had to be called in on March 21.

The Tatas looked after ten thousand refugees over seven months in specially designed camps. The overall responsibility and supervision of the medical care for the migrants was given to Pesi, and he had to undertake almost daily visits to the camps early in the morning before going to the hospital and late in the evenings before going home.

When Bihar suffered a severe drought in 1965 and 1966, Pesi led the medical relief work in Bihar. The drought was largely responsible for wildfires in the area and created major health problems and death from lack of access to clean drinking water, poor air quality, and a surge in heat-related as well as respiratory illnesses such as asthma. Stagnant water, from reduced water levels in wells and lakes, provides a breeding ground for disease-carrying mosquitoes and other insects resulting in outbreaks of malaria and filariasis.

Filariasis can affect the lymphatic system, causing a condition called elephantiasis, which is characterised by soft tissue swelling, commonly seen in the legs, but it can also affect the arms and genitalia, with resultant disfigurement and disability. The affected individuals were often shunned by the community and abandoned by their families, eventually ending up as beggars.

In years to come, Pesi was to operate on many of the unfortunate victims of this disease, surgically excising the excess soft tissue and performing skin grafts and repairing the secondary hydroceles that were a common sequelae in advanced cases.

In April 1979, Jamshedpur witnessed communal violence between Hindus and Muslims. The Hindu festival of Rama

Navami was being celebrated with a procession through a Muslim neighbourhood when someone threw a stone and violence erupted, leading to several days of rioting and bloodshed that caused casualties on both sides.

This is a report from *India Today* (https://www.indiatoday.in/magazine/special-report/story/19790515-more-than-100-lives-lost-in-jamshedpur-communal-riots-822018-2014-02-26):

In the neighbouring Pakistan General Zia-ul-Haq executed the former prime minister Zulfikar Ali Bhutto (April 4th 1979) without any bloodshed whereas in India more than 100 lives were lost in communal rioting that took place in the steel city of Jamshedpur.

The outbursts took place almost simultaneously, beginning on the early afternoon of April 11 and continuing through the night to grip most of April 12 as well. It was as if by some remote control mechanism the entire city burst into flames....

.......Syed Idaullah, a Telco worker, whose house and brother's tailoring shop on the main street have been reduced to cinders, with only the charred remains of sewing machines and a bicycle, was ferreting for left-overs when he told India Today: "At one moment there was a shouting, restive mob. Then almost instantly, I saw smoke bombs which I thought was tear gas, but realized that there was open shooting."

On April 12th an ambulance containing women and children who were being taken to safety was set ablaze by a frenzied mob, killing forty occupants. This incident took place in Bistupur which is the main shopping centre in Jamshedpur.

During this time TMH provided relief with the doctors, nurses and other staff, forgoing leave and willingly giving up their spare time to work around the clock, looking after the wounded and injured.

Pesi worked round the clock, organising and supporting the relief teams and medical staff, and during the worst of the carnage, he actually slept in the hospital to show solidarity for the staff and be available in case his advice or expertise was required.

For the excellent care he had provided and the organisation of the relief teams, a special commendation was conferred by the Bihar State and Central Governments as well as one from the Minorities Commission.

Pesi's leadership earned him enormous respect, affection, and trust from his colleagues and the staff at Tata Main Hospital. He was a firm believer in the saying, "What is bad for the hive is bad for the bee," and constantly boosted the morale of the exhausted staff by telling them that they were all in this together. This was never more so than in a crisis. He exhorted the hospital staff not to give in to hopelessness, even in the face of overwhelming numbers of casualties, not all of whom could be saved. "You have stood up, when things have broken down. You have tried your best to help. Each of you, from the cleaners to myself, is playing their part, to ease suffering when we see it and make the world a better place. By helping one another to do their tasks, we are protecting the people we care most about."

Pesi felt that it was important to use this terrible time, not just to help as many victims as possible but also within the hospital—to help his colleagues, junior doctors, and nurses to learn new skills—and in doing so, he built lasting relationships.

He believed that being the head of TMH was about fostering a community within the institution as well as caring for the health needs of the community outside it. Even though Pesi went on to have a long career after he retired from Tata, the Tata Main Hospital (TMH as he always referred to it) was his life's work.

2 BC Road Jamshedpur

Gool (far right) standing next to famous gynaecologist Dr Masani, Mrs Masani & Pesi in Jubilee Park 1966

Pesi in his 2 BC Road home 1966

10

Chief Surgeon and
Superintendent of TMH

True worth is in being, not seeming,-
In doing, each day that goes by,
Some little good, not in the dreaming
Of great things to do by and by.
For whatever men say in their blindness,
And spite of the fancies of youth,
There's nothing so kingly as kindness,
And nothing so royal as truth.

—Alice Cary

WITH PESI WORKING long hours at the hospital and
the arrival of their new baby daughter, Gool resigned from
her job and became a homemaker. She kept her registration
with the Bar Council and stayed in touch with her profession

by reading law journals and also did freelance consulting work, giving advice to clients and drafting legal notices and letters.

Pesi was now on the governing council of the Jamshedpur Blood Bank and the Jamshedpur Eye Hospital, as well as on the visiting committee of the Government Hospital, Jamshedpur.

In 1968, Pesi and Gool had their second child, a boy named Zarir. The same year saw the arrival of the Naxalite movement in Bihar. This took the form of violence by Maoist revolutionaries called Naxalites. The word Naxal comes from a place called Naxalbari in West Bengal, the birthplace of the movement. It was an organised revolt based on the ideology that power grows out of the barrel of a gun and sought to fight feudal tyranny and exploitation of the poor and deprived members of society by means of violence. Originally founded in 1967 in neighbouring West Bengal, by the following year it had spread all over Bihar.

It was commonplace to see gunshot wounds, stab injuries, and burns brought to the casualty in TMH, and Pesi spent long hours in the operation theatre dealing with victims of violence.

The Tata group had a philosophy of philanthropy and this extended beyond their own employees. When there was a major train accident near Jamshedpur because of a derailment, the hospital was opened up to all the injured, and all casualties were treated free of charge.

Yezad Kapadia recalls having four of his fingers nearly severed with an axe. He was driving home late one night and opened the door of his garage to park the car. He was shocked to see a small group of people surrounding a man, with one of the group holding an axe aloft—as if about to behead his victim. As soon as Yezad opened the door, the man made a dash for it. Yezad immediately tried to shut the door on the attackers, but the axe came down on his hand, slicing his fingers open. He was rushed to TMH and Pesi was summoned to repair the damage.

Some years later, intruders broke into Yezad's house and shot him in the chest with a pipe gun. It was the middle of the night, and while Yezad was rushed to hospital, a messenger was despatched to Pesi's house to fetch him. Yezad made a full recovery. He had penetrating chest injuries, with some of the bullets lodged within the lungs. Pesi decided that the risk of trying to remove the bullets was too great and left them untouched, preventing any infection by giving intravenous antibiotics.

In December of 1971, there was a military confrontation between India and Pakistan over the liberation of East Pakistan (now Bangladesh), which led to war between the two countries. In March of 1971, riots erupted in Chittagong.

"Operation Searchlight" was ordered by the central government in West Pakistan, to take control of all major cities in East Pakistan and eliminate politic and military opposition. They met with strong and prolonged resistance during which 300,000 to 3,000,000 civilians were killed and ten million refugees fled to India. Kishanganj district in Bihar is flanked by West Bengal in the east as well as to the north. A narrow strip with a width of just over 12 miles separates it from what was then East Bengal, now Bangladesh. Refugees poured into Bihar through Kishanganj and relief camps were set up. Pesi organised medical relief for the refugees in the Kishanganj area, organising medical supplies, setting up clinics for medical treatment, and lobbied for food, clean running water, and sanitation, which were vital to prevent an outbreak of infectious diseases.

After the communal riots in 1964, migration from East Pakistan to India continued, and Pesi had felt the need to organise formal relief efforts. The Indian Red Cross Society in Bihar was established in January 1970 with support and encouragement from Tata Steel, with many of their executives signing up as volunteers. The St John's Ambulance brigade provided humanitarian relief and gave medical aid during the Bangladesh liberation war.

With their 1st child - Azmy - Pesi & Gool

Pesi in St John's Ambulance uniform - Bangladesh war

With Mr Nanavati - Bangladesh War

Dr Pramathanath Dey St John's Ambulance Brigade Jamshedpur with
Dr Datta Anaesthetist TMH

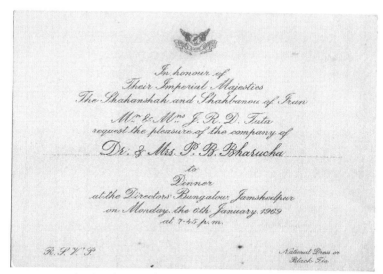

Invitation to dinner with the Shah of Iran

11

Mera Machine Theek
Kar Deejiye
(Please Put My Machine Right)

"**DOCTOR *SAHEB, MERA*** machine *theek kar deejiye*," pleaded the strapping Pathan patient in casualty.

The machine in question being his erect penis, over which he had managed to slip a metal nut—presumably when it was in the flaccid state. However, the resultant penile swelling was such that he was unable to remove the metal ring, which was lodged at the penoscrotal junction, occluding the blood supply to his organ and causing unbearable pain and inability to pass urine. This is a condition called ischaemic priapism—a state of prolonged penile erection, caused in this case due to blood not being able to leave the penis.

The casualty officers had already tried lubrication in an effort to slip the nut off—without any success and much to the patient's distress. A ring cutter used for removing tight rings had proved ineffective against the thickness of the metal nut. One of the junior doctors had suggested that the patient should run up and down stairs with the object of diverting blood away from the penis and thus reducing the swelling and achieving detumescence, but by this time the man, who was prostrate with distress and unable to stand, started screaming, "*Bada* Doctor *ko bulao*" (call a senior doctor).

The patient was right to worry about his machine. Ischaemic priapism is a medical emergency. The blood trapped in the penis is deprived of oxygen. When an erection lasts for too long, this oxygen-poor blood can begin to damage or destroy tissues in the penis. As a result, untreated priapism can cause erectile dysfunction.

Pesi looked at the turgid penis, the skin now discoloured, and realised he had to act fast. He wondered about a surgical saw to cut through the metal but this would risk damage to the skin. The quickest and simplest way would be to aspirate the blood from the penis, reducing the swelling, but this would have to be done under anaesthesia in the operation theatre.

Using two needles inserted into each corpus spongiosum (the erectile tissue which contains most of the blood), about 50 ml of dark blood was evacuated, the aspiration continuing till bright red blood was seen, and once the penis was relatively flaccid, the nut was slipped off the shaft. There was an audible sigh of relief in the theatre and the assistant surgeon breathed, "Well, done, Sir!" Pesi was aware that the blood vessels might fill up again and it was important to position the penis properly to prevent this from happening. He gently bent the penis over the scrotum so erection could not occur, and this position was maintained by compression dressing and binding in the shape of a T. An indwelling catheter was placed in the urethra as the patient would not be able to pass urine spontaneously for the next few days. After five days, the bruising and swelling had settled, the catheter removed, and the man passed urine without difficulty.

He was discharged with instructions to avoid sexual intimacy for the next six weeks. He arrived for follow up two months later in good spirits and reported that his machine was in excellent working order.

12

Cometh the Hour, Cometh the Man—
Pesi's War on Smallpox

"CHECHAK," "SITALA" **OR** *"Shitala,"* or *"Badi Mata"* (Big Momma) is what small pox was called in Hindi. Small pox is a highly contagious viral disease characterised by fever, weakness, and a skin eruption with pustules that either result in haemorrhagic disease or slough off, leaving permanent scarring. Smallpox has a mortality rate of 30 percent. This is higher in infants and young children.

It gets its name from the Latin word for "spotted," referring to the raised, pustular bumps that break out over the face and body of those affected. Those who survived were often left blind, sterile, and with deep pitted scars, or pockmarks, on the skin.

There have been smallpox outbreaks across different parts of the world for centuries past. The death tolls were so large that it was often likened to the Black Plague.

Jamshedpur is located in the Chotanagpur plateau and in 1974, when the region was gripped by a smallpox epidemic,

Dr. Pesi Bharucha was Senior Surgeon, Superintendent and Chief of Medical Services of TMH. The collieries and mines in Dhanbad and Naomundi were also under the umbrella of the Tata Main Hospital, which was the referral centre for the entire area.

At the time, Jamshedpur was in the state of Bihar. Today it is in the state of Jharkand, which was formed in November 2000.

Donald Ainslie Henderson (September 7, 1928–August 19, 2016) was an American medical doctor, educator, and epidemiologist who directed a ten-year international effort (1967–1977) that eradicated smallpox throughout the world and launched international childhood vaccination programs. In his book *Smallpox: The Death of a Disease*, pp.177–184, he describes the problem THE DARKEST DAYS OF ALL— JANUARY TO JUNE 1974.

"My feelings of despair during the first six months of 1974 are etched in memory.

Yet another catastrophe
In late April, formerly smallpox-free areas in India began to report smallpox outbreaks—primarily among labourers. These workers had come from a major railway centre and industrial complex, Jamshedpur (population 800,000), in southern Bihar. By early May, 125 such notifications had been received; and ten to fifteen new ones were arriving daily. Jamshedpur was the major industrial centre for the Tata Industries heavy industrial manufacturing group. Officials of the company immediately offered help in organizing and conducting an intensive search and vaccination program

throughout the greater municipal area. More than 2,200 cases were found. To keep the disease contained, all railway travellers were vaccinated before departure; bridges and major roads were barricaded. Only those who were vaccinated were allowed to pass. It took two months before the outbreak was controlled. Eventually, the government and Tata Industries reached an agreement for Tata personnel to assume responsibility for the program throughout southern Bihar state. From the Jamshedpur epidemic alone, 300 additional outbreaks and 2,000 cases had occurred in eleven states of India and in Nepal.... Mr. J. R. D. Tata, approved expenditures of $900,000 for the provision of personnel and vehicles."

Mr R.M. Lala writes in his book *The Creation of Wealth, The Tatas from the 19th to the 21st Century* (Pages 179–182):

"The Chotanagpur division of Bihar (now Jharkand) is a vast area of 65,000 square kilometres, larger in size than either Punjab or Kerala.....

The region consists of forests, ravines, valleys and wooded hills. Above this area are studded thousands of villages and some major towns like Ranchi..., Dhanbad, the coal centre of India; and Jamshedpur, the city of steel. Over eleven million people reside in this area of whom one-third are adivasis (tribals).

In 1974, this division of Chotanagpur became the epicentre of a small pox epidemic. The World Health Organization (WHO) and the government estimated that between January and June 1974, 6,000 lives were lost through small pox, apart from many thousands crippled by the disease.

A couple .... in Japan were found to have small pox and it was traced back to Tatanagar station. Dr Nicole Grasset, head of WHO, New Delhi, rushed Dr Larry Brilliant, an expert from the USA to Tatanagar for personal investigations. WHO, had a few years earlier, launched its campaign to eradicate small pox and this outbreak came as a great disappointment... ..

If tackled vigorously at this stage, WHO believed that small pox could be eradicated by 1976. ....."

Dr Brilliant had a tall order. He requested Tatas' help to have fifty doctors, two hundred para-medical supervisors, six hundred to nine hundred vaccinators-cum-searchers of the dreaded disease, fifty vehicles and innumerable other facilities.

.... Doctors were drawn from the main hospital in Jamshedpur...with .....Dr Pesi Bharucha, chief co-ordinator (Medical). ....The staff recruited had to be trained within seventy two hours in vaccination and the essentials of small pox control and containment. It was a round-the clock operation. Come the seventy-two hours the teams were on the road.

In a fortnight four hundred outbreaks were discovered within the 4.5 mile radius of Jamshedpur and lakhs were treated with vaccination as part of the containment strategy. It was not smooth sailing either. The adivasis preferred to worship the goddess Sithala and visit the medicine man. One tribe refused to permit the doctors and vaccinators to touch their people until they had been given the green light from their great leader. The problem was that the great leader happened to be in hiding with a price on his head! A small team of Tata officers had to go blind-folded, transferred from one jeep to another and then taken by road to the hideout of the chief. The chief gave his permission orally and the Tatas had to tape record him, return to the villagers in the area and play back the tape to convince the tribals that the great man had given permission.

Evenings were preferred by vaccinators because the menfolk were home from their fields. One day, an innocent vaccinator had knocked on the door of a tribal hut. When the door opened, two tribal ladies equipped with darts and arrows charged at the poor vaccinator, who ran for his life. Within six weeks the area was declared by WHO to be under control.

Though Tatas immediate responsibility was completed, Dr Brilliant appealed to the Chairman, JRD Tata, for help of the field organisation that had been built up to tackle the entire division of Chotanagpur which included eighty-two towns and 20,500 villages. The time scale of the operation was six months. The Tata Steel Board met and sanctioned the project.

The second phase of containment was launched with fifty-six teams fanning the entire area. This operation stretched the resources of Tatas to the limit, some of its finest officers went at some risk to remote areas in forests where hygiene was unheard of. Dr Pesi Bharucha, the superintendent of the hospital, recalls that in these far-away places they could often take only three items of food. The first was a dish of tea, where tea, milk and water were boiled on a stove but nothing was strained for fear of infection. The second was chapatties which were picked up and eaten fresh from the fire. The third dish available was boiled potatoes. There were "flies, flies, flies everywhere". Often in the late evenings, as the sun set upon the wild forest, Dr Larry Brilliant would turn to Bharucha and say: "Now, Doctor, where shall we go for dinner tonight? To the Sheraton or to the Hilton? You name it and I'll come with you." Invariably, the two tired doctors and their small team would settle down at a village tea shop on packing cases to their three-course meal. There were instances where entire teams got lost in the jungles and once the Tata Steel plane had to search for a team that had not reported back for two days. ....”

Another dedicated and highly skilled doctor who was part of the team was Dr Pramathanath Dey, Medical Officer in Plant Medical division of TISCO at the time, a position he held from 1961–1993. His daughter—Swati remembers him returning home weeks after being sent out to remote areas surrounding Jamshedpur. Being the peak of the Indian summer, without electricity or running water, this was a harrowing experience and Dr Dey found that vaccination and treatment was the easy bit; the challenge lay in convincing the villagers and tribals who were almost always illiterate, to accept immunisation, and treatment. They had their own fixed, firm and invariably false beliefs about illness and disease with superstitions related to treatment. Many tribal women would hide infected infants on the thatched roofs of their huts and cover them with watermelon creepers to avoid detection.

Nevertheless, Phase II of the operation was declared highly successful.....

WHO wanted Tatas to go the extra mile and join Phase III, namely of consolidation. If this phase was successful the cherished dream of WHO of eradicating the menace from the world could be achieved. ...ending June 1975......a message came from WHO, New Delhi, that India was free from the first time in history from indigenous smallpox. In May 1980, WHO declared that small pox was eradicated from the world.

Russi Mody, Managing Director of Tata Steel....wrote. “Those who have been involved in the campaign from the beginning have had the rich experience of sharing the sorrows of the downtrodden and poor, of the neglected and forgotten segment of society. Perhaps by their efforts a line in the history of mankind has been written.....”

Dr Pesi Bharucha worked night and day during the 1974–1975 smallpox campaign. Totally in charge of the Tata teams eradication work in the Chotanagpur division which at the time constituted roughly one fifth of the geographic area of the State as well as its population, during this period his wife and children aged nine years and six years, did not see him for weeks and till he returned home tired, hungry, sweaty and dusty, they had no idea if he was well, leave alone alive. . There were no facilities for bathing and to answer the call of nature, they had to make their way into the undergrowth at the edges of the forests. There were no telephone connections in most of the villages and no running water or electricity. In the spirit of the Tatas, and his readiness to make sacrifices for the common good, given the circumstances of the time, he embodied and put into practice the values of the Tata group and the needs of the community he served. None of the doctors received or sought any extra remuneration for the long hours they put in or for the weekends with their families that they sacrificed.

Pesi never boasted or sought fame and recognition, never complained or felt that as a highly skilled surgeon, he should not be sent out into the wilds to run a vaccination programme. Nevertheless, in honour of his great contribution to the eradication of small pox:

a. A special commendation was made by the Bihar State and Central Governments.

b. A commemorative plaque was presented to him by the Regional Director of WHO for South East Asia.

c. A commemorative plaque was presented to him by Dr Karan Singh, Minister of Health and Family Planning, Government of India.

d. Fellowship of the Indian Society for Malaria and Communicable Diseases was conferred in recognition of the significant contribution and practical work.

With JRD Tata

Greeted by Karan Singh - Health Minister

In New Delhi for National Award

Seated next to Dr Brillant

Dr Pramathanath Dey

Dr Dey CPR training

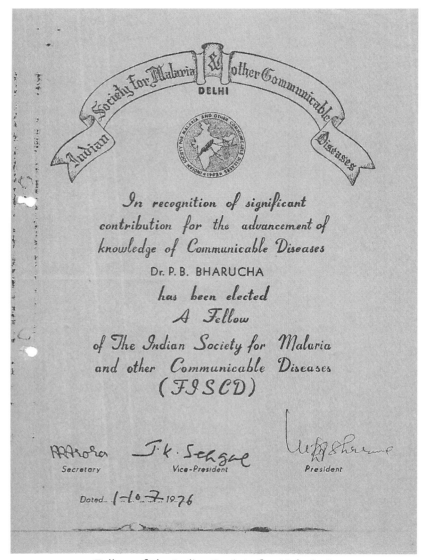

In recognition of significant
contribution for the advancement of
knowledge of Communicable Diseases

Dr. P. B. BHARUCHA

has been elected

A Fellow

of The Indian Society for Malaria
and other Communicable Diseases

(FISCD)

Secretary

Vice-President

President

Dated 1-10-7-1976

Fellow of the Indian Society for Malaria &
other Communicable diseases

Pesi with Christiaan Barnard

Pesi with nurses at TMH

13

Thumbs Up!

Azmy and Zarir,
The reason I today have ten functioning digits on my two hands
is because Pesi Uncle refused to give up on me . . .

The story of my severed right thumb in 1975 has become part of
TMH folklore . . .

Everyone had given up and told me to start practicing using my
left hand as my right thumb, though reattached, was just a black
lump of dead flesh . . . But not your dad . . .

Jamshed Surti recollects the story of the severed thumb:

Once upon a time . . .
Being an accident prone kid, I would end up in the emergency
ward with various cuts and bruises. The nearest available
neighbour, Aunty, usually Sheroo Aunty or Rati Aunty, would
have the distinctly uncomfortable job of having to ferry me
to the emergency room and stay with me till my mum, who

worked across town in Telco, could make her way to the hospital. Usually the attending doctor would handle it with lots of Mercurochrome and a shiny new white bandage. Ninety-nine times out of a hundred, Bachoo Aunty, Nikoo Aunty, Noshir Uncle, Xerxes Uncle, and everyone else who worked at the hospital would have popped in to see what the latest wound was about and to try to make me stop crying.

As a kid, I remember this great big man would appear and, suddenly, everything would be all right. He had a really strong, firm grip and the coolest pair of hands, courtesy probably from the air-conditioned operating theatre from where he tore himself away, before the Surti kid brought down the whole hospital. Pesi Uncle commanded the room when I was a five-year-old kid and even though the last time we met, he was bedridden and well into his nineties, he still had that same incredible presence and ability to command the room. During every drive to and from the hospital, Pesi Uncle's house would be pointed out.

I was probably around eight years old when I presented Pesi Uncle with one of his "biggest challenges of his career as a surgeon." His words not mine.

While the large homes in which we lived, with the huge gardens and backyards filled with trees, had all the cooking done on gas, the domestic help relied on little balls of charcoal dust and *gobar* (cow dung), which were meticulously assembled. All the cooking for the domestic help and their families were done on these little stoves into which these little balls were loaded and set ablaze. Having one of the trees shed a dead branch here and there was a godsend as burning wood meant getting time off from the time-consuming activity involved in "assembling" the charcoal and *gobar*.

One particularly rainy afternoon, one of the two gulmo-har (flame of the forest or flame tree) trees that defined 10 Beldih Lake shed one of its giant branches. The branch fell half inside and half outside, across the barbed wire fence. The cracking sound of the branch breaking had everyone in the area rushing to collect as much of it as they could. I too rushed out to see what all the excited shouting was about.

The first task was to drag the entire branch in before the "outsiders" laid claim to their stake since it lay on a public road. Jamuna, who was working with us as a domestic help and my favourite, warned me to stay inside the boundary as they all went out to push the branch in. There was absolute pandemo-nium as the branch was heaved into the compound. The little kids were accumulating the twigs and the seed packets, the older ones were snapping the smaller branches and hauling them away. I saw a thick part of the branch and decided to "save it" for my favourite Jamuna. This involved me putting my arm over the top, which was way above my sight line.

Unfortunately, I was outside the sight line of Elizabeth (Sheroo Aunty's very deaf servant) who, standing on the other side of the branch, had already swung the axe.

There was no pain, just a numbness that gripped my entire right arm. I don't remember who screamed first or louder. I just stood there with blood spurting out of my thumb. Someone grabbed my hand and wrapped it in the first piece of cloth they could find which happened to be someone's *"gamchaa"* (a traditional, thin, coarse cotton towel). Everyone knew the drill. "Sheroo memsahib *ke pass le chalo*." (take him to Sheroo Memsahib). Sheroo was the wife of Dr. Noshir Piroshaw, the dental surgeon who lived next door to the Surti family.

I remember being bewildered as I was hauled off to our beloved neighbour's house through the gap in the fence. Sheroo Mom, as she was fondly called, also reeled at the sight of me being hauled in to her spotless kitchen, with my arm held firmly above my head in a rag soaked with blood. I was promptly sat up on the counter and Sheroo Mom told me to look away as she inspected the damage. I remember her gasping and I thought, I must have really outdone myself. The spotless kitchen towel turned red in a second as Sheroo Mom dragged me out the back gate, to a waiting pedal rickshaw which had been summoned.

As there was only place for the two of us, Sheroo Mom sat me in her lap as she continued to hold on tightly, trying to staunch the bleeding. The last thing I remember before passing out was her encouraging the rickshaw puller to do his best up the slope from the Blood Bank to the TMH main gate.

The first face peering down when I came to was Pesi Uncle. Inside the operating theatre there were others but none that I recognised. Strangely, there was still no pain.

By then, my parents had arrived along with a whole bunch of concerned aunties. One of the things about growing up in Jamshedpur was the sense of community. It was on full display that day and the weeks and months that followed.

The next day, Pesi Uncle came to visit me and inspect and change the dressing, which covered my hand from the wrist down. For the first time, I actually got to see my thumb. It was weird. It had turned completely black above the knuckle. There were strings poking out of the black bit. Pesi Uncle turned my hand to show me the thin sliver of skin by which it had dangled, till he had stitched it back on. By this time all the excitement had worn off. So I hopped out of bed and opened the door with my injured hand, or so I was told.

That was it! I was promptly shipped off to the emergency section under instructions from Pesi Uncle, and a cast was slapped on, which covered my forearm and wrist. This was the solution, they thought, to keep the arm immobilised and give the thumb a fighting chance to heal. Needless to say, the cast was extended right up to my shoulder before the week was out.

While Pesi Uncle would reassure me what a big, strong boy I was growing up to be, I was petrified of needles. Back in those days, the way to take a blood sample was to have the top of your finger stabbed by what seemed like a sewing needle and then some blood was squeezed out. In the mind of an eight-year-old, with no reassuring Pesi Uncle around, this procedure was unbearable.

Poor Rati Aunty was on "Jamshed watch" when the attendant came around to collect the blood sample. I was told that besides running around and hiding under the bed, I had also threatened to yank off my freshly-sown-back-on thumb, rather than have that needle stab me on the tip of a finger. Needless to say, Pesi Uncle was summoned and the world returned to normal.

By this time, a couple of weeks had passed and school was being missed. Homework was brought to the hospital, but with my right arm in a plaster cast up to the shoulder, it remained largely ceremonial as there was no writing possible. The mass that was once the top of my thumb remained stubbornly black. Weeks turned into a month. I was instructed to start figuring out how to write with my left hand as hope was fading for the blood supply to ever return to the "dead" thumb.

While everyone from my parents, siblings, and the entire community were convinced that I would have to start from scratch with my left hand, that was not so with Pesi Uncle.

On a daily basis, he came, peered at my thumb, poked and prodded, and reassured. Almost two months into the episode, I gave him the answer he was looking for as he held my hand. "I can feel you scratching the top of my thumb." Both my parents cried and my siblings joined in, though I am pretty sure they were as clueless as I was about the emotion attached to feeling at the top of an appendage declared dead by all, except one.

While my thumbnail never grew back, every visit to Pesi Uncle would start with an inspection of the thumb. Forty years down the track, he grabbed my arm from his bed and inspected it before asking how it was functioning.

What Pesi did:
He was aware that total thumb amputation constitutes a major loss of hand function (40 percent disability to the hand). Jamshed was a right-handed eight-year-old with his life ahead of him. Moreover, the Surtis were like family, having taken care of Pesi's daughter Azmy like one of their own when Pesi and his wife had taken their four-year-old son to the UK for surgery, just two years previously.

Jamshed had his thumb almost completely amputated through the middle, severing both neurovascular bundles and flexor tendons. It was apparently attached by a strip of dorsal skin and extensor tendon.

Today, with the development of delicate surgical instruments and the operating microscope, surgery of tiny blood vessels and replantation of severed digits can be performed with excellent results, but Pesi had no access to an operating microscope.

The saving grace was that there was a bridge of tissue—skin and tendon between the partially severed thumb and the hand—and this gave the surgeon hope. He remembered his surgical training, reminding himself that as long as there was some continuity of tissue, there is persistence of blood supply to the injured digit. Also, this was a sharp injury caused by cutting, which had a better prognosis, versus a crush injury or an avulsion injury where the thumb is torn off.

Jamshed was taken for surgery less than an hour from the time the injury took place, so his thumb was not deprived of its blood supply for very long.

Pesi needed to debride the wound first, followed by bone fixation and tendon, blood vessel (artery and vein), and nerve repair. All this was done by the naked eye, in the absence of an operating microscope. The surgery lasted nearly five hours.

Consent was given by Mrs. Sheroo Piroshaw and by the time Jamshed's parents—Silloo and Eruch Surti—arrived from work, he was already in the operating room. The faith they placed in Pesi was both humbling as well as frightening.

The staff recall that one of the few occasions that they had seen Dr. Bharucha lose control was when, a few days later, Jamshed—having recovered from the anaesthetic and the initial shock—decided to explore the room using his right hand and then announced his intention to see if the thumb had indeed been properly sewn on by yanking on it with his left hand. The nurse on duty, the poor "aunty" (all older ladies, family friends, neighbours, and friends' mothers were aunties in those days) on duty, the junior doctor on the shift, and Jamshed faced the full force of Pesi's wrath. Jamshed was rushed down to the treatment room and his right upper limb completely immobilised in a cast.

Once his hand had returned to normal, one of the first things he wrote was a note to his surgeon: "Thank You, Pesi Uncle for saving my thumb."

Jamshed's right thumb

14

Pesi Realises His Dream—
A Brand New Hospital

TMH STARTED OUT as a "cottage hospital" (a small rural building with several beds). When he took charge of TMH after Col. Lasrado, he worked hard to develop orthopaedics, paediatrics, obstetrics & gynaecology, radiotherapy, and dental surgery.

It was always his mission to have a purpose-built multispeciality hospital to meet the challenges of a changing world—with the latest medical advances, bringing research into practice, and informing clinical leadership with radical ideas and critical thinking. In 1964, this goal was simply an aspiration.

Since becoming superintendent of TMH, Pesi had led the evolution of the hospital and created a solid platform for future developments. He had led the expansion in stages, till it reached a capacity of 600 beds with separate surgical, medical, maternity, gynaecology, and paediatric wards. There were dedicated speciality outpatient clinics as well with radiology, ophthalmology, ENT, dermatology, and rehabilitation medicine. Despite this, it often fell short of meeting demand, and Pesi had expressed a need for expanding the hospital as soon as he became superintendent.

Support for this plan came originally from Sir Jehangir Ghandy and later from Mr. R. S. Pande, who had been a director in Tata Industries since 1964, the same year that Pesi was promoted to chief surgeon and superintendent of TMH. In 1970, Mr Pande became a full-time director in charge of administration and sales, and was then promoted to managing director in 1972. Both Sir Ghandy and Mr. Pande had great respect for Pesi as a doctor and asked Rumy Master, the chief architect of TISCO at the time, to help with the planning, design, and construction of the new hospital. Rumy and Pesi visited various hospitals in India together, carefully planning and preparing a blueprint.

Finally, after years of planning, the five-storey, 256-bed Sir Jehangir Ghandy Memorial Hospital (JGMH) with six operation theatres was commissioned in 1975. It was purpose built on an eleven-acre site adjacent to the TMH, with a floor space of over eighty square foot per patient, specially calculated to ensure better circulation of air and prevent cross infection. There was a designated "common room" in each ward for patients to relax and read or play a board game while convalescing and a visitor's area where relatives of the more seriously ill patients could rest. Each ward had its own service unit, with a doctor's room, a room for the nurse, and a pantry with access via a service corridor so the patients on the ward were not disturbed. A separate, fully air-conditioned three-storied "operating theatres" block housed six operation theatres, a plaster theatre for orthopaedic cases with anaesthesia and recovery rooms on the top floor, a central sterilisation unit, conference room and library on the first floor, and a central kitchen on the ground floor to provide hygienic meals for the hospital patients. At the time of opening, the JGMH was the most modern of its kind in India.

Pesi had invested an immense amount of time and effort into this endeavour, purely out of altruism, as he always worked towards improving the care of patients in the town. Looking back, he never quite understood how he reconciled the competing demands of work and family.

He did not really reap the rewards of his own work as he retired in 1980, just a few years after the JGMH came into being.

Pesi with JRD Tata - model of future multispeciality hospital

All India Congress O&G Pesi seated centre

Inauguration of JGMH

Pesi with Rumy Master in Darjeeling

15

Retirement from TMH: A New Chapter in a New Place—What Pesi Did

IN SEPTEMBER 1980, Pesi turned sixty, and in accordance with the rules of TISCO, he retired from his job.

Gool and he had decided to move to Bombay; their children were now fifteen and twelve years of age and Gool wanted to return to work. Pesi was offered positions at the Jaslok, Breach Candy, and Masina Hospitals in Bombay.

At the invitation of Lady Soonu Jamshetji Jeejeebhoy, who was a trustee of the Masina Hospital in Bombay, Pesi accepted the position of an honorary consultant surgeon at the hospital, which he attended from 1981 to 1985. In 1982, he was approached by the Breach Candy Hospital Trust and took over as Medical Director, a position he held till 1996.

Pesi continued his clinical work till he was sixty-five, when he retired from Masina Hospital and focused on being the medical director of Breach Candy Hospital. The hospital needed to expand, and Pesi was keen that an extension and a new wing should be built to accommodate more patients and provide a wider range of diagnostic services. The MRI department was established during his time at Breach Candy Hospital and, at his personal request, TISCO donated steel at concessional rates to help with the construction of the new wing. Pesi was always keen on the advancement of medicine and it was at his initiation that a research centre was created.

As a result of his connection with the Tata group, the Tata head office in Bombay often approached him to oversee the care of their employees from all over India. He was trusted so much, that often, whatever the nature of the problem, before any specialist opinion was sought, Pesi was the first point of call. In 1986, as a personal favour to Pesi and the special relationship he had with the Tata group, Russi Mody, chairman & managing director of TISCO, sanctioned a sum of two million rupees as a donation to the hospital.

Pesi's deep involvement in all aspects of the hospital's working earned for him the enduring respect and admiration of the staff, patients, and trustees alike. He served as medical director of Breach Candy Hospital for just over fourteen years and during this period brought in a lot of changes, both in terms of additional facilities for patient care and in the variety of medical expertise he introduced within the hospital. He had a unique knack of understanding and interpreting the needs of the medical staff and taking these to the board of trustees. Possessed of innately humane qualities, he dealt sensitively and tactfully with patients and their relatives, dealing with complaints fairly. With his vast experience, seniority in the medical profession, and clinical expertise, the consultants often came to him when they had interpersonal difficulties or patient-related issues. His advice and guidance was particularly helpful in medico-legal cases.

At the end of his tenure, Pesi had obtained recognition from the DNB (Diplomate National Board) for postgraduate doctors to train in different specialities within Breach Candy Hospital. The hospital needed a postgraduate librarian and he recruited trained staff so the library stayed open for twelve hours a day. When he first came to the hospital, the medical records were housed within the library. He created a separate department for medical records, upgrading the quality by insisting on proper documentation of case notes and correct indexing and filing.

A departmental library was created with input from the heads of departments in various specialities.

Pesi finally left Breach Candy Hospital at the age of seventy-six. He continued to work after he left, providing consultancy services in hospital management to hospitals in New Delhi and Hyderabad as well as serving on the National Advisory Board of the Aware Cancer Hospital in Hyderabad.

GEN-2/20 Pads/2-85

BREACH CANDY HOSPITAL
AND
RESEARCH CENTRE

60, Bhulabhai Desai Road, Bombay-400 026. – Telephone : 822 36 51

27th May 1987

The Chairman & Managing Director
Tata Iron & Steel Co.
Bombay House
Homi Mody Street
Bombay – 400 023.

Dear Sir,

    I seek your indulgence by mentioning a few facts about the Breach Candy Hospital. It is run by a Board of Trustees drawn from different walks of profession and business. The hospital finances are managed by the fees earned from the general public and from donations. The hospital does not have a corpus. Diagnostic, preventative and curative treatment is available to patients without distinction or race, religion, caste, creed or any sectarian consideration.

    As of today the hospital has 100 beds, and 25 beds for the under-privileged who are treated without any payments (excepting for their meals and charges for special drugs in some cases.) The hospital provides the same standard of health care to the free patients as to the paying patients. The same doctors, nurses and paramedical staff serve the Charity Wing as they do the nursing patients.

    The demand for medical facilities in the Metropolis of Bombay has increased tremendously. Without exaggeration I can say that Breach Candy Hospital offers perhaps the best medical care in Bombay. Our Board of Trustees are very keen to increase the existing bed strength and services. With this in view, we are embarking on additional accomodation for 66 beds and associated infrastructure facilities. We have just received clearance from the Government as well as the Bombay Municipal Corporation to proceed with additional construction of approximately 25000 sq ft. In about 10 days time we will be embarking on our new construction for which we have gathered some funds.

........2/-

Letter from Pesi to Tatas

112

GEN-2/20 Pads/2-85

BREACH CANDY HOSPITAL
AND
RESEARCH CENTRE

60, Bhulabhai Desai Road, Bombay-400 026. – Telephone: 822 36 51

: 2 :

On behalf of the Hospital Trust, I earnestly request you to help us by donating at least half of the quantity of steel needed for our new construction which is approximately 40 metric tonnes :-

TOR steel (Tistrong)   32.80 tonnes

25 mm = 4000 kgs

20 mm = 2500 kgs

16 mm = 10200 kgs

12 mm = 6000 kgs

10 mm = 1500 kgs

8 mm = 8600 kgs

Mild steel   7.2 metric tonnes

6 mm diam 7200 kgs

Before concluding this appeal, may I take this opportunity to thank TISCO for their help in our past ventures, and await their generous donations for the current expansion.

Assuring you of our best attention at all times,

Yours sincerely,

P.S.

Donation to the Breach Candy Hospital enables the donor the tax concession under section 80G of Income Tax Act.

/ 27-5-87

DR. _____ M.D., F.R.C.S.
DIRECTOR

Letters from Pesi to Tatas Page 2

THE TATA IRON AND STEEL COMPANY LIMITED

BOMBAY HOUSE, 24, HOMI MODY STREET, FORT

BOMBAY 400 001

Ref: G - 2517

11 June 1987.

Dr. P. B. Bharucha,
Director,
Breach Candy Hospital and Research Centre,
60, Bhulabhai Desai Road,
Bombay 400 026.

Dear Dr. Bharucha,

Donation of steel for new construction

      Kindly refer to your letter dated 27th May, 1987, addressed to our Chairman and Managing Director requesting for donation of steel for new construction to be taken up for additional beds at the Hospital.

      We are glad to inform you that, as recommended by Mr. S. A. Sabavala, we have sanctioned the supply of 40 (forty) tonnes of reinforcing steel at a concessional price for the purpose. The concession will be at the rate of Rs.200/- per tonne, on the actual quantity of reinforcing steel for which purpose you may kindly approach the Company's Regional Sales Manager at New India Assurance Building, 148 Mahatma Gandhi Road, Bombay 400 001.

                            Yours faithfully,
              THE TATA IRON AND STEEL COMPANY LIMITED

                    (J. C. Kalele)
                  SENIOR EXECUTIVE OFFICER

TELEGRAMS: IRONCO · TELEPHONES: 2049131-2048453 · TELEX: II-2618 & II-2731 TATA IN

Donation of steel for new construction at BCH

Pesi with VP Singh - PM of India 1989 - 1990

16

Recognising the Beat:
A Devastating Diagnosis

PESI HAD BEEN medical director at Breach Candy Hospital for some years, when he received a letter from his dear friend and erstwhile colleague Noshir Piroshaw. Noshir's wife Sheroo had been complaining of strange symptoms for several months. She had noticed that her petticoats were getting tight and her waistline was expanding, even though her intake of food remained the same. A peculiar rash appeared on her face and body, shedding flakes of skin over the floor, and had to be swept up and cleared away. And most recently, she had developed weakness in her legs, which made walking difficult. Noshir told Pesi that she had consulted different doctors and been told to go on a diet and to exercise, but now her physician felt she ought to see a neurologist and also a dermatologist. Would Pesi be able to see her first, he asked, for the "apex opinion" as Noshir always referred to Pesi's diagnosis. Whenever there was a diagnostic conundrum at TMH, invariably Pesi would be approached.

So it was on a hot summer afternoon that Noshir and Sheroo, accompanied by their younger daughter Zavher, came to the Medical Director's Office. Sheroo narrated all her symptoms again and confessed that she was feeling generally unwell and so tired that she would lie down most of the day, getting up only when she heard Noshir sounding his horn to announce that he was home from work. Not wanting to worry him, she had said nothing, but now she was finding it hard to walk.

Pesi requested Sheroo to lie down on the examination couch and, in his usual way, began a systematic examination, starting with the head and neck and working his way down. After examining the abdomen, he said, "Noshirwan, you are barking up the wrong tree. She has severe ascites." Ascites is the medical term used for abnormal fluid build-up in the abdomen. The rash was dermatomyositis, which is a rare inflammatory skin condition associated with muscle weakness. It has a strong relationship with cancers of the breast, lung, and ovary. Pesi explained to Noshir that rather than a dermatology or neurology opinion, Sheroo should have an ultrasound scan of the abdomen and also a CT scan for more detail.

The results of the scans were devastating. Sheroo had advanced ovarian cancer, which had spread beyond her ovaries into the abdomen. Noshir was broken; Sheroo and he were extremely close and he loved her dearly. Sheroo had been his rock, the anchor for him and the two girls. Everyone was gutted by the diagnosis.

Pesi had always reminded his colleagues and junior doctors never to miss the "BEAT":

B—for bloating
E—for eating difficulty—feeling full more quickly
A—for abdominal pain or discomfort
T—for toilet changes (in urination or bowel habits).

These symptoms get worse as the tumour grows and spread beyond the ovaries, making it much harder to treat. Because the symptoms can be vague, they are easily dismissed, which is what had been happening to Sheroo.

Ovarian cancer is a silent killer, in that the symptoms are non-specific and often ignored, which is why he had always exhorted his colleagues not to miss the common symptoms. Pesi always felt that it was more "quiet" than "silent"; symptoms tend to be subtle, which women often ignore and doctors sometimes fail to recognise. "Always examine the patient properly, rather than just eliminating a cardiac or neurological condition. You are treating a patient and not the respiratory or gastrointestinal system," he would tell his juniors time and again. Women diagnosed in the earliest stages of ovarian cancer have double the chances of surviving for five or more years.

Sheroo and Noshir's daughter Zavher recalls the moment when her mother was informed of the diagnosis: "I remember that moment vividly. In Samudra Mahal. I also remember the moment Daddy saw Mummy's CT scan/MRI report in the ante-room of your Daddy's clinic. His secretary was there. Daddy started weeping. She consoled him. Then we went to the guest house at Samudra Mahal and he told my mother. He stood facing the window looking out at the vast expanse of the sea and wept. My mother put her arms around him. I watched silently, shattered."

However, Russi Mody, the managing director of TISCO, sanctioned funds for Sheroo to have treatment at the Memorial Sloan Kettering Cancer Centre in New York. After undergoing major surgery, Sheroo received chemotherapy and did reasonably well for three years, after which there was a recurrence of the cancer. Always cheerful, always smiling, and never complaining, Sheroo lost her battle against the disease in 1994, passing away in her own home with her family by her side. Noshir adored his wife and felt shattered after she had gone. However, he continued his work at the hospital but as he always said, he missed her every minute of every day.

Dr Noshir Piroshaw with his wife Sheroo
& younger daughter Zavher

17

The Ravages of Time and a
Stroke of Misfortune

AFTER HIS RETIREMENT from Breach Candy Hospital at the age of seventy-six, Pesi continued to be active for a few years. He was asked to provide advisory and consultancy services for new hospitals that were springing up in different parts of India, and he travelled to New Delhi and Hyderabad.

However, a knee replacement operation which did not go well restricted his mobility. Things had never been right from the start and within two years, it was obvious that the implant was mal-positioned and would have to be taken out, so he underwent revision surgery, which left him with a shortened leg on one side, a limp, and dependence on a walking stick.

A corneal ulcer in his left eye needed a graft, which failed, and he was left partially sighted. Nevertheless, he remained cheerful and upbeat through all of this, travelling to visit his daughter in the UK, three years in a row, to help through her pregnancy and also when she had her baby boy—Pesi and Gool's first grandchild.

In 2008, just ten days before his eighty-eighth birthday, Pesi had a stroke and was admitted to Breach Candy Hospital. By this time, Gool was beginning to show all the signs and symptoms of dementia, and Pesi was constantly concerned about how she would manage if anything happened to him.

The stroke affected his left side but he was left with his speech, cognition, and vision intact. His eighty-eighth birthday was spent in Breach Candy Hospital where he insisted that the staff were given *jalebis* (an Indian sweet) and *samosas* (pastry stuffed with potato).

When his neurologist came to check on him in hospital and began to examine the muscle strength in the left shoulder, Pesi corrected him by reminding his physician that the arm had to be fixed at the side in order to make a proper assessment. Pesi had a long hospital stay but worked hard with his physiotherapist and left the hospital walking with a frame.

However, there was a slow decline after this, both for him as well as for his wife. Gool became progressively more forgetful, often aggressive, displaying behavioural and psychological symptoms of dementia. Having no insight into her condition, she refused treatment and frequently quarrelled with the carers that Pesi needed day and night. Despite this, Pesi remained the head of the household, providing calm and logical reason, smoothing over difficulties. But all the while, he was crumbling physically, gradually becoming less mobile till at the end, he was wheelchair bound.

He had an immensely upbeat temperament, bearing all his afflictions without complaint. Whenever anyone phoned to ask how he was, the reply would always be, "First Class!"

Sometimes, when asked if he was keeping well, he would reply, "As well as you can expect someone in his nineties to be." In all of the trials and tribulations he endured in the last ten years of his life, Pesi was a shining example of how to accept events and situations that cannot change. He displayed a perfect understanding of how to really just be content with what he had.

Even in that final decade of his life, Pesi found happiness and enjoyment in his two younger grandchildren—Eva and Kian—whom he loved dearly and insisted were the spitting image of his own parents—Bachoobai and Behramsha Bharucha. People who commented that Eva looked like her mother were promptly corrected by Pesi insisting that Eva did not look like *her* mother, she looked like *his* mother.

Finally, on November 28, 2018, Pesi was summoned by his maker and died in his own bed at home with his daughter Azmy and his dear friend Noshir Piroshaw's daughter Zavher by his side.

His last few days are described by Azmy below in a message to her friends:

Dearest Friends,
I apologise for not acknowledging all your messages, sent so promptly and sincerely after my father died on the 28th November.

I meant at the time, to respond to each one of you individually but unfortunately, in an attempt to free up data on my phone, I have deleted them. Hence, this letter to the entire group.

They say that bereavement rewrites your address book, you realise who is there for you, who cares enough to reach out, and I feel so privileged and touched by the outpouring of thoughts, messages, prayers, and calls I received after my father's passing.

So many of you have experienced loss yourselves, one or both parents, some of you at an earlier age than others.

My father lived to a ripe old age. He died at the age of 98 and went peacefully. Most of you remember him as a doctor and surgeon at TMH in the 1970s. People have spoken about his skill and expertise as a surgeon and clinician.

But, he was, above all, a kind and caring person, a good human being who treated people with respect, whatever their station in life. He was a good husband, brother, friend, and father and, as were all our parents, a thoroughly decent person, in every sense of the word. As George Eliot put it so well in *Middlemarch*: "The growing good of the world is partly dependent on unhistoric acts and that things are not so ill with you and me as they might have been, is half owing to the number who lived faithfully a hidden life and rest in unvisited tombs."

In September 2008, a week before his 88th birthday, Dad had a stroke which took away his independence but he bore this with grace and fortitude. As time went on, he grew progressively more frail but never protested, never railed against the indignity of being bathed, cleaned, dressed, and toileted by carers. Every time I called and asked how he was, the reply was, "First class." There is an old saying that adversity tests the brave and my father's resilience is an embodiment of a verse in the Corinthians: " . . . my strength is made perfect in weakness . . . in distresses . . . For when I am weak then I am strong."

I arrived in Mumbai on the 26th November and he was very weak, the beginnings of a bed sore appearing in his sacrum;

he kept bring his hands together as if in prayer 🙏 and pointing up ☝, indicating that he wished to depart this world. He stopped eating and drinking the following day, asked to see "my son," told us to look after Gool (my mother) and then on the 28th, suddenly became restless in the afternoon. "Time *thaiee gayo*" (in Gujarati, the time has come). He held my hand and whispered in my ear, "I want to go to God." I said he could go, he had lived a good life and there was nothing to be afraid of. His breathing changed and it was as if he had been given a general anaesthetic, he slipped into a state of coma, there was no gasping, no change in colour, and a minute or two later he passed on.

There have been so many beautiful and moving verses written about death—Shakespearean sonnets, Greek poetry, songs, and essays. My brother Zarir and I have not been able to reach an agreement on which one of them best captures the end of my father's life and perhaps we never will because each life and each passing is unique. I don't think "all the trumpets sounded for him on the other side" as John Bunyan describes in *Pilgrim's Progress* but I prefer to think of his departure as Death describes that of Hans in the *Book Thief*. "His soul sat up. It met me. Those kind of souls always do—the best ones. The ones who rise up and say, 'I know who you are and I am ready.'"

My brother and I were so privileged to have our father. We are thankful to dear friends and family who have remembered him and sent kind and loving condolences.

The book of memory is filled with joy and although there is nothing more to write, it can still be read.

We wish you and yours all the best for 2019.

Pesi on his 94th birthday

On navjote of his grandson

Zarir's engagement, Pesi & Gool with Zarir, Niloufer(Zarir's fiancee) & Azmy

Zarir's wedding day

Pesi with his attendant Arti at his son Zarir's engagement

Pesi a few months before he died

18

Condolence Messages;

Memories of Pesi

JAMSHED SURTI:

Azmy and Zarir,

The reason I today have 10 functioning digits on my two hands is because Pesi Uncle refused to give up on me...

The story of my severed right thumb in 1975 has become part of TMH folk lore...

But that is not what I remember as my most vivid memory of the man who was more like a Father to a lot of us.

Maybe Zarir can back me up on this one.

When I was in college in Mumbai in 1987, I had a really bad crash on my motorbike late one night. Scars of which I still carry today.

I ended up calling your dad as it happened on the Breach Candy-Peddar Road cross . . .

He came to Breach Candy, where he was boss at the time and personally cleaned me up. I remember Zarir was there and he looked terrified as half of my skin had been torn off my arm, shoulder, back, and hip.

Pesi Uncle ensured he did everything himself He sent me home and told me not to worry..

When I went to meet with Gool Aunty and Pesi Uncle, he asked me how everything was with a very knowing look. This was just a few years ago.

Even though he looked frail lying in his bed, he was sharp as a tack. He even tried to explain to your mum, who mistook me for my dad.

Even though we may have dispersed to all corners of the globe, we are and will remain Family. Bound together no, by the joy of our childhood filled with so many moms and dads in Jampot.

Lots of love and hugs,
Jamshed

YEZAD KAPADIA
Azmy and Zarir dear,
I had to transfer this write up from my mobile to the computer to read it. I know of almost, but not all, the incidents you have mentioned.

You need to know that he once saved my life. When Jeroo and Ruki were very small, some thugs broke into my house and shot me with a pipe gun in the room where the girls were sleeping! About 100 pellets were pumped into my body. All Jamshedpur, including RHM, was alerted. Dad did not pick up the phone as he had taken sleeping pills because he had taken his mother-in-law to the station late at night. Someone had to be sent to his house to call him. He came at once. He could remove most, but not all, the pellets at first shot. A second attempt was made to remove others. But by then flesh had grown over the pellets and they kept shifting their position, which made it extremely difficult for him to operate. About five pellets entered my lungs and still remain there. I was given strong doses of penicillin to prevent infection. He wanted to open my lungs to remove them but decided against it. Years later, when over 90 and I was visiting him, he inquired about the pellets!!

I was once attacked with an axe, which nearly severed four fingers of my left hand. He was summoned from a party at Ninny Vakil's place to operate on me. They needed 20 stitches!!

Being in Jamshedpur, Rati was a bit nervous when Ruki was to be born. Pesi told her I will be there holding your hand when Ruki arrives. He, with Dr. Kapadia, the gynae, were at a party at Sir Jehangir's house. Both of them left the party, so they that your father could fulfil his promise to Rati.

That was your father. He led a life truly along Gathic principles. Both Zarir and you should be proud to have had a father like that.

Wishing both of you well for the future.

Yezad
Azmy,

Another one for your Dad's Story.
Sir Jehangir Ghandhy, the uncrowned King of Jamshedpur needed to have his prostate removed. He could have gone to the best of urologists in any corner of the world but insisted that Pesi perform the operation at the TMH. Although Pesi did call for a specialist urologist from the Patna Medical

College to assist him, he performed the operation very successfully himself.

Y

I distinctly remember the first occasion we met. I had been operated for appendicitis before leaving for Jamshedpur and was having a tingling sensation in the scar. I called Pesi for an appointment. He came punctually. I was pacing up and down in front of his room. He had yet to take over as Head of the TMH. After a careful examination he reassured me that the wall of the stomach was strong and that there was nothing to be afraid of.

He left all engagements to come to the hospital wherever I or Rati needed him—for the shooting (lead pellets in the chest), axing of my left hand, Ruki's birth, also the time I was gassed in the plant. His presence was always reassuring.

He always chuckled when he related the story of the strapping Pathan who, for some strange reason, managed to slip a nut over his erect penis and could not get it out!!. Pesi was told "Dr. *saheb, mera* machine *ko theek kar do*!"

He got a rousing farewell from the Company when he retired, in complete contrast to other officers who were either not given a farewell or did not want one!! A reflection of how well he was respected by the Company.

He was always held in high esteem by both his junior colleagues Drs. S.B. Singh and K.P. Mishra

He was always there for people whenever he was needed.

These are random thoughts as they occurred to me. They will have to be put in perspective.

Will try and send other anecdotes, as and when I remember.

Yezad

FROM COUSIN NEVILLE JAVERI

Dearest Azmy and Zed:

I feel I didn't get enough time with either of you to share my emotions and sentiments on the passing of dear Uncle Pesi. My earliest memories of your dad are ones of an incredibly kind, large-hearted, and generous man who happened to be one of my favorite people. Zed, I remember him watching us set up your stereo system at Paradise and when we realized we were missing speaker wires he drove us to Sukh-Sager so he could buy them so that we could finish setting up. I am sure he realized how excited we were at the time and didn't want to have us feel let down by having to wait another minute/hour. Given that we were just a bunch of kids and he could have had so many others things to do, he still made the time right there and then to warm the hearts of a couple young kids.

He was more than just an uncle to us; he was a caregiver and a support system for my entire family. My mom and dad were always surprised by his unexpected visits to our home when he had heard that Rashna or I were unwell. They were unannounced and full of concern and caring. There was a true genuineness that flowed through him—one that didn't ever need to be put on or practiced. I remember cutting my foot which led to an infection; he asked me to come over and changed the dressing for ten straight days till it was healed; he helped set Rashna's arm when she dislocated it, all the while distracting her so she wouldn't focus on the shock or discomfort. Later, when my dad was ill, he remained a source of strength to us and in particular to my mom who was having a hard time dealing with the stress of it all. When my father passed away, Zed, you came to receive me at the airport and we talked about our parents—at the time you mentioned that your dad was not keeping particular well. Later that morning I attended the first set of prayers for my dad—they started early in the morning—before 8:00 a.m. At one point I happened to look up and there was your dad— in a wheelchair attending the service. He later made it a point to tell me that he thought my father was a special individual and could have nobody but well-wishers and friends. When I think back to that conversation I think of Pesi Uncle and think that he must have armies of friends and well-wishers. If there ever is a Heaven, he is seated in the inner council.

I last saw him a few months ago—again he was kind and good enough to make the effort to come have lunch with family at The Willingdon Club. I could see then that he had turned more frail and weak. We still had a nice conversation—there were some moments I didn't follow quite what he was trying to say but all of sudden the band started playing Sinatra's "My Way." Your dad seemed to absolutely enjoy the music and when the song ended he pounded the table enthusiastically in applause. It was a moment and memory I will cherish forever.

I felt I had to share what I was feeling on his passing. I was traveling when I got the news and it has left me hollow. The world lost one of its finest but another place has gained exponentially. Please accept my prayers and karma and know that I will cherish having called your dad "my uncle" as one of my greater gifts that life bestowed.

Neville

SVATI KANIA
Dear Azmy! I just saw the announcement about your father. I am so sorry for your loss. He was a gem of a man—they

don't make them like they any more. He truly supported my family in many different ways—a genuine and kind friend. I know he will find eternal peace. Lots of love to all of you. 🙏

ZIYA TARAPORE (NEE GANDHY)

So sorry to hear of your loss, Azmi! Pesi Uncle was one in many millions!!

RIP!

MEHER POCHA (NEE SEERVAI)

My dear Azmy

I have just seen this—we were in Eltham visiting Jehangu's stepmother and got home rather tired after being in a traffic jam caused by an accident on the A-1 M

Your father must have been a wonderful man. I knew him as "Gool's husband" and was only vaguely aware that he was medical. Whenever we met he was quiet and unassuming and one would never have realised what a talented and effective man he was. Thank you for sending the obituary—it opened my eyes.

For you it must be a sad loss, even though he had reached a good age. You must all be proud of his many achievements.

Jehangu joins me in sending our deepest sympathies to you and your family. I don't have Zarir's e-mail address—please would you pass on our condolences to him as well. What about your mum? Once before when I wanted to phone her you said she had difficulty dealing with phone calls.

Love,
Meher

ANWAR HASAN
Heartfelt condolences. Great man and a very good human being. Recall with nostalgia the time he was in charge of TMH and I was heading the Town Division. We used to jointly work out our replies to The Union's questions. Memorable days.

Missed out on a century! But he had a good life. May he rest in peace.

Anwar.
NEERA MISRA

Azmy
This is Neera Misra. I am so very sorry to hear from Anita about Pesi Uncle's passing. My childhood is full of memories of him, your Mom, Zareer, and you. When we were moving to the US, we had to get a medical exam done in Mumbai. There was some confusion and I went and met with Uncle and he got it resolved so we could get the exam done and get back to Nasik the same day. Just this weekend I was telling my kids about how Alka and Bunty stayed with you all during the JSR riots.

For me Uncle represented the last of that very fine generation of TMH doctors. I've not come across any with that same sense of caring, professionalism, dignity, and ability to command respect and confidence.

My deepest regards to Gool Aunty, you, and Zareer at this tough time in your lives.

DIPIKA JANKINATH LAL
Dear Azmi
Sorry to hear about Pecy Uncle. My dad & uncle were so fond of each other. He was such a kind and helpful man. I can't

forget how much trouble he took to make my spine surgery successful & problem free at Breach Candy conducted by the best doctor in the world, Dr. Ralph Claword. May God give Gul Aunty & you all strength to bear this irreparable loss.

HARBHAJAN CHADHA

My contact with Dr. Bharucha was that of a doctor administrator and a patient. Let me describe him in one sentence. Dr. Bharucha was a gentleman doctor. Difficult to say which side was heavy. He was a competent surgeon and during that period, a general surgeon used to perform all kinds of surgeries. He used to do this with perfection. He had no air because of this and talk to all, patients or their attendants or employees of hospital in very gentlemanly and satisfactory manner. I thought gentleman doctor would be the right word for him.

I had direct contact with him 4 times, 3 of those around 1970 in Jamshedpur and 4th in Breach Candy, Bombay, now Mumbai in 1986.

My mother was diagnosed with high blood pressure (220/120) by Dr Kavi at South Park dispensary. We were advised to admit her in TMH. We rushed her to TMH and got her admitted. She was put in Gen ward as cabins in those days were very few. Neither she nor me were happy as there was little privacy there. It was past 7 p.m. A little disappointed, I was moving out as I saw Dr Bharucha, head of TMH, opening the door of his car in front of his office to go home. I moved a little faster to reach him and he noticed that as he sat in his car. As I reached near his car the gentleman doctor took the key out and came out. I explained to him the situation. He told me that no cabin is vacant, but he would help me and he walked with me to the ward and told the sister to move my mother to special ladies ward, where there were only 2 or 3 beds. I did not know of this ward. Before I came out to thank, he was gone.

Another instance, I had bleeding along with stool in Delhi while on leave. I showed to a competent senior doctor there. He diagnosed it as fissures and advised operation. Back in Jamshedpur, I showed it to Dr. Bharucha in OPD. I told him about the Delhi surgeon's advice. Without any comment about Delhi advice, he suggested a cream for applying in the affected area and told me in his usual mild tone, operation is not required. It is about 50 years now, that advice has worked and valid.

In the 3rd instance, my domestic help broke his leg. He got on a tree and slipped. I got him x-rayed and was advised to get the leg plastered. I was told it was not serious. I proceeded to work and told him that I would take him to a private doctor in the noon when I come back for lunch. He was not a TISCO employee. He however got himself admitted care of one of his employee relations. The leg was plastered next day and after 3 days on discharge his relation was told to pay the bill for treatment of non-employee. It came to a few thousand rupees. His relation now came running and requested me to help.

I went to Dr. Bharucha and explained to him the situation. I told him that ultimately, it will have to paid by me. He again helped me to get that treatment charged as a poor patient, which was hardly anything. He never told me that I was approaching him again and again.

In 1986, I was advised heart bypass surgery. Mr. K. C. Mehra, Vice President TISCO, sent me to Breach Candy

Hospital, Bombay for advice. Heart surgeries were, at time not that common and risk was much higher than at present. Dr. Bharucha was head of Breach Candy at that time. He rang up Dr. Dallal, a young cardiologist, and fixed up an appointment. He explained to me that I will have to cross the road for reaching Dr. Dallal's clinic and in Bombay I have to go step-by-step forward to cross the road. I could see he was still not satisfied and came out of office and explained to the taxi driver the way and also to accompany me for crossing the road. I cannot forget that guardian like feeling of him.

May his soul rest in peace.

I have given the description of the facts in simple language. Probably it could have been better described. You may edit it if you so desire.

Best wishes,
H. L. Chadha
B 389, Sarita Vihar,
New Delhi 110076
Tel. 9911294140

Printed in Great Britain
by Amazon

47473916R00092